AN AD
FOR MURDER

JOHN PENN

CHARLES SCRIBNER'S SONS
NEW YORK

Copyright © 1982 John Penn
First published in Great Britain as *Notice of Death*

Library of Congress Cataloging in Publication Data

Penn, John.
    An ad for murder.

    I. Title.
PR6066.E496A3   1982   823'.914   82-10761
ISBN 0-684-17761-7

3 5 7 9 11 13 15 17 19 F/C 20 18 16 14 12 10 8 6 4 2

Printed in the United States of America.

CHAPTER 1

For a moment he was shocked—stupidly shocked, perhaps—but shocked nevertheless.

Tom Cheryl stared resentfully at the advertisement. Thursday was Aileen's day for the local Women's Institute, but before leaving she must have folded the newspaper and propped it carefully against the toaster so that it would be the first thing he saw when he sat down to breakfast. Otherwise he might have failed to notice it at all; he normally passed quickly over the book pages. He wondered why she had bothered and supposed she had thought it a joke. Somehow he didn't.

Major Thomas Henry William Cheryl, DSO, formerly of the Royal Engineers, lived in retirement in the Oxfordshire village of Farlingham with his wife, Aileen, and his boxer bitch, Sal. He was sixty-three, grey-haired, blue-eyed, army-moustached, tall and straight-backed—still a most attractive man. Axed in one of the defence cuts some years ago, he had discovered an unsuspected and surprising flair for business. Ten years in the City had ensured a generous supplement to his pension, and he had then retired again, this time voluntarily, to lead a pleasant and placid life in the country.

At least, it was usually placid and pleasant. This morning he wasn't so sure. The advertisement was absurd, of course, but it still left him feeling vaguely uneasy.

He turned to the financial pages and began to study them as he started on his eggs and bacon. But he found it hard to concentrate. Neither the dollar rate nor the rise in the price of gold nor the fluctuations of the Dow-Jones average seemed as important as they normally did. A report on the bankruptcy of a firm in which he had once held an interest caught his eye, but even this failed to hold his attention.

He put his plate to one side and poured himself another cup of coffee. The general news was much the same as ever — wars and rumours of wars, a flash flood in India, a revolution in Central America, devastating fires in California — everywhere death, or the threat of death, from natural causes or man-made. Against his will he turned again to the extraordinary advertisement.

Technically, though the Major didn't know it, it was a display ad in a prime position, a double-column box, 10 centimetres deep, bordered with a wide black rule, and placed at the top right-hand corner of the right-hand page of the double-spread of book reviews and publishers' announcements. The text, set in a bold sans-serif face, read: 'Coming Soon — THE DEATH OF MAJOR CHERYL'.

That was all. It was presumably advertising a book, but there was no publisher's name. No trademark or colophon. No author. No price or indication of its content. That information would undoubtedly appear in later ads. This was just to attract the reader's attention — a 'teaser', he believed they called it in the trade. But he wished to hell they hadn't chosen his name to tease with!

Irritably pushing back his chair, Major Cheryl stood up. 'Come on, Sal,' he said. 'Walk. Good for both of us.'

The boxer had been lying on the floor, half asleep, but she gave a low growl and got slowly to her feet. She was eight years old and less spry than she used to be, but she was still a good companion. Another dog wouldn't be the same. The Major pulled himself up sharply. Couldn't he think of anything but death this morning?

Mrs Hodgeson, who came in three days a week to clean, was in the kitchen. The Major called to her that he'd be gone for an hour or two, let himself out of the house and set off with Sal. As they reached the bottom of the drive, he looked back at his home. It was no mansion, but a pleasant, large detached house with plenty of garden — a 'stockbroker's residence', he supposed it might be called. Its neighbours in the quiet road on the outskirts of Farlingham village were of a similar character, but varied in design; the nearest was perhaps fifty yards away.

They turned into the road, Sal straining at her lead, but hadn't gone far when a car drew up beside them. A head poked itself out of the window.

'Morning, Major. How are you?'

'Fine, thanks. And you?'

The local doctor was grinning broadly. 'You certainly look all right — for one who's soon about to leave us.'

'What do you mean?'

It was a pointless question. He knew perfectly well what Dr Carson meant. It was that damned advertisement. He wondered how many of his friends and acquaintances would read it or hear about it.

'Haven't you seen the morning paper?'

'Yes, I have,' said the Major shortly.

'Then you saw —'

'I saw it — if you mean that announcement about some book or other. It's nothing to do with me. Fellow just happened to pick my name, that's all.'

'It's not a particularly common name.'

'Nonsense! Hundreds of Cheryls round the country.'

Luckily at this point Sal lost interest in the scent she had been investigating, and began to tug at her lead. It was an excellent excuse. With a wave of his hand the Major continued on his way.

He hadn't gone a hundred yards when, passing the church, he was accosted by the vicar. One profession after another, thought the Major. But, unlike Dr Carson, who was not one of his favourite people, the Reverend Edwin Galverstone was a friend, and Tom Cheryl stopped fairly willingly.

'Hello, Edwin. Could you do with some pears? My trees are bowed down with fruit.'

'Any you can spare. We can always bottle them for the lean months. Many thanks, Tom.'

For a while the two men talked gardening. Then Sal grew impatient again, and the Major said he must be off.

'Goodbye, Edwin. See you on Sunday. Make it a nice short sermon.'

'Goodbye. Take care.' Suddenly the vicar grinned. 'Very special care. What have you been up to, Tom? Why's someone threatening you so publicly?'

The Major groaned. 'Not you, too,' he said. 'Does everyone in Farlingham read that blasted paper?'

'Quite a few, I imagine. And the ones that don't will get told. In fact, Nina Dawlish mentioned the advertisement to me. I met her in the Post Office.'

'Then I'll change my mind. I was going to buy a few stamps, but I think I'll give the High Street a miss this morning.'

'I should. It's full of visitors anyway. Sometimes I regret we've become such a centre of interest.'

Tom Cheryl nodded his agreement. When he and Aileen had first moved to Farlingham it had been a quiet and peaceful village with few strange faces. Then one of the pubs had been taken over by new people, who tarted it up and made it famous for its food. The church's Norman past was rediscovered, and the village's proximity to better-known Cotswold beauty spots. Farlingham found itself on the tourist map—'small, but not to be missed', according to one guidebook. So, in the summer, the place was often overcrowded. The Major, like most of the older inhabitants, preferred it as it had been.

For this reason he never went near the Golden Hind, except on a few occasions when he was with Aileen or some of her county friends. He preferred to drink at the

Duck and Drake, a simple country pub with no frills, known locally as 'The Birds'. Situated at the far end of the village, it made an excellent half-way house on his daily walks with Sal.

This morning, having cut across the churchyard and completed a two-mile circuit through the lanes, he went into it as usual. He was early but already, as well as the publican and his wife, half a dozen customers were assembled. They were all local regulars and, as the Major entered, conversation stopped abruptly.

'Good morning, everyone.'

The response was ragged, almost uncivil. Tom Cheryl frowned. He glanced questioningly at the publican, who stitched a smile across his face.

'Morning, sir. The usual?'

'Please.'

He walked across to the bar to pick up his pint of beer. Leaning on the counter, he noticed the newspaper on a lower shelf. He sighed. During his walk he had met no one he knew and he had almost forgotten the advertisement. Now he was forcibly and unpleasantly reminded of it. He realized that the coldness of his welcome at 'The Birds' was solely due to embarrassment. They had been having a good yatter about him, and he had interrupted them.

He glanced casually around. There were Davies, the verger, and old Mr Marchant, and the Carver twins who did odd jobs around the neighbourhood, and another elderly couple whose name he couldn't immediately call to mind. He doubted if any of them opened a book from one year's end to another. And that went for the publican and his wife, too. Certainly they never read book pages and book reviews. But someone had noticed his name today and they were, very naturally, curious.

Tom Cheryl was basically a shy man. After his meetings with the doctor and the vicar he had realized that some chaffing was inevitable; there was no point in resenting it. But he hadn't bargained on being treated as a kind of marked man by the whole village. He drank his beer quickly, nodded to the publican and strode out, Sal at his heel. If the old fools wanted to gossip about him, let them do so in peace.

He had another drink when he got home, and ate the food that Mrs Hodgeson had prepared for him. He spent the afternoon in the garden, mowing the grass and digging over a bed for some late vegetables. These were soothing occupations. Later he made himself some tea and sat on the terrace in the sun. He was there, dozing, when his wife returned.

Aileen Cheryl was ten years younger than her husband. A tall, thin, not unhandsome woman, she suffered from an excess of nervous energy. She ran her household with great efficiency, led a busy social life and was an unflagging worker for an indiscriminate array of good causes. But she was admired, rather than liked. Though she was considered a devoted wife and mother, it was many years since she and Tom had shared a bedroom, and both her daughters had left home as soon as possible — Celia to marry an American and live in New York, and Jill to follow a teaching career in London. Aileen merely worked harder.

'Tom!' Her voice was sharp with exasperation. 'Do you know the time? We're due at the Dawlishes for drinks at six-thirty and you haven't changed yet. You can't go in those old gardening things.'

'Sorry. I must have dropped off.'

Tom Cheryl got up, stretched and yawned. The Dawlishes had lived nearby for some time, in a very large Cotswold stone house a few miles outside the village. Aileen seemed to find them good company and was especially friendly with Nina Dawlish, but he had little in common with them and had no desire to go and drink with a crowd of people he didn't particularly like.

'I'm stiff after all my digging,' he said. 'I think I'll have a long hot bath.'

'Tom, there isn't time. Didn't you hear what I said? The Dawlishes are expecting us and—'

'I know. I heard. But I don't want to go to the Dawlishes. You go, Aileen. Make my excuses. Say I'm not feeling well or something.'

'All right.' Aileeen was on the point of turning away when she suddenly stopped. Her expression changed. 'Tom—that is just an excuse, isn't it? I mean, you aren't really feeling ill?'

'No, of course not.' He was surprised. He and Aileen had an unwritten understanding about such things. Unless it was a matter of importance, to say that one didn't wish to do something was enough; the other didn't question it. 'Why do you ask?'

'I—I don't quite know. Because of that extraordinary advertisement in the paper this morning, I suppose. People usually don't feel well if—' She laughed, but without humour. 'Silly of me. After all, it's only a book—nothing to do with us.'

'Nothing.' Tom Cheryl agreed, but he remembered that it was Nina Dawlish who had told the vicar about the ad. He was glad he'd decided not to go to her party.

The next day was Friday and on Fridays Tom Cheryl went into Oxford, the nearest large town. It took him about forty-five minutes and it was a pleasant drive, if there wasn't too much traffic and Aileen didn't want the Jaguar.

On this particular Friday he set off in good spirits. Concentrated on emerging safely from his drive, he paid scant attention to the motor-cycle that was parked a little way along the road and began to follow him at a comfortable distance.

The weather was perfect, warm but not humid, a light breeze, a blue-grey sky above scudding white clouds, and the hedgerows fresh after the night's shower. The big car purred along.

The Major noted subconsciously that the motor-bike in his rear-view mirror had accelerated as if to overtake him, but took no action. They were on a straight stretch of road and there was no approaching traffic. It was a sensible place to pass.

Then the unexpected happened. Without warning the motor-cyclist swerved, cutting in on the car so that for a second or two there were only inches between the rear of the bike and the Jaguar's front bumper. Instinctively Tom Cheryl braked hard and swung the wheel over. The car slid sideways across the road, scraped along the hedge and finally came to rest by a tree. The Major was breathing fast.

'You bloody fool!'

He shook his fist after the fast-receding motor-bike. Of course the fellow hadn't stopped, and there had been no chance to get his number. All he could recall was a fleeting glimpse of a yellow crash helmet and black leathers. The man was a maniac. He'd quite deliberately forced the Jaguar . . . Suddenly mindful of his car Tom Cheryl climbed out and inspected it. There was little damage, only a nasty scratch along the side of the bodywork, but Aileen would not be pleased.

Swearing volubly the Major got back into the car and reversed from the hedge. He was a little shaken and definitely angry, but he was not in the least fearful. The incident was over, and it never occurred to him to connect it with yesterday's mysterious announcement.

The Major drove on to Oxford. He left the Jaguar in a car park near Gloucester Green, and went straight to a department store in the centre of the town for morning coffee. Later he would do some desultory shopping, and finally drive up the Banbury Road to lunch with his sister. His Friday routine varied little and had been established over the years. Its very consistency made him vulnerable.

Half an hour later the Major emerged from the store's glass doors opposite the Martyrs' Memorial. He hesitated, and then joined a small group waiting at the edge of the pavement to cross the street.

There was a steady flow of pedestrians behind him. In front, the road was busy with traffic. Several cars went by, then some bicycles and a truck, hooting loudly. A double-decker bus was lumbering towards the group. As it came almost level, Tom Cheryl felt a sudden sharp punch in the small of his back.

The Major lost his balance. He flung out his arms but there was nothing he could do to save himself. He was falling into the street, directly in the path of the oncoming bus. He caught a glimpse of the driver's terrified face and was aware of heat from the engine and the immediate threat of big, black tyres. A woman screamed. Then someone had seized him round the waist and pulled him to safety. They fell together in an untidy heap on the pavement.

A small crowd gathered round them, helped them to their feet. The driver was climbing down from the bus, visibly shaken. A policeman was approaching. There was a babble of conversation.

'He could have been killed.' 'Right under the wheel.' 'If it hadn't been for this young man . . .' 'The driver wasn't to blame . . .'

Tom Cheryl took a grip on himself. He had caught one knee a nasty whack on the kerb but was otherwise unhurt. He turned to the man who had saved him. 'Thanks,' he said. 'I'm very grateful to you.'

'That's okay, sir.' A young man with fair hair and bright blue eyes waved a dismissive hand. He was already edging away. Apparently he wanted no publicity.

Nor did Tom Cheryl. 'I'm sorry,' he said to the policeman and the bus driver and the other people gathered round. 'I'm sorry. It was very careless of me. I just slipped on the edge of the pavement. It was an accident.'

It had to be an accident. But not on his part. He hadn't been careless. He hadn't slipped. Tom Cheryl's thoughts were grim. First that stupid bugger on the motor-bike, and now this . . . He collected his car and, disregarding his intended shopping, drove towards his sister's house. He could still feel the punch in the small of his back. If that young man hadn't been so quick to grab him . . . He told himself not to be fanciful. It was only that blasted ad that made him think like this. What was that silly saying—'Once is happenstance, twice is coincidence, the third time it's enemy action.' This was mad. There would be no third time. There was no reason on earth why anyone should want him dead.

CHAPTER 2

Tom Cheryl didn't mention his close shave with the bus to anyone—not even his sister. The limp resulting from his badly bruised knee he explained away as a touch of rheumatism. And he lied about the Jaguar. He told Aileen that he'd found the long scratch on its side when he returned to the car park; some unknown careless driver hadn't even had the decency to leave his name and address under the windshield wiper.

He spent a quiet weekend. Aileen had asked a few friends in for sherry after church on the Sunday, and he had to stand a little chaffing about the advertisement, but by now the joke was beginning to wear thin. Naturally no one connected Aileen's story of the scratched car with any threat to his life.

Just as he went into Oxford every Friday, Tom Cheryl spent almost every Tuesday night in London. Nominally his weekly visits were concerned with business—he still held one or two directorships in the City—and Aileen had never sought any further explanation. She wasn't really interested. She seemed to accept that he stayed at his club on Tuesdays. To his knowledge she had never checked, though he always left a phone number with the porter for use in an emergency. Given the circumstances, the arrangement was ideal, and Tom Cheryl treasured his Tuesdays.

By the time Tuesday came, he himself had begun to doubt whether any threat existed. The motor-cyclist could easily have misjudged his speed and distance; many of them rode wildly just for the hell of it. The push in the back could have been accidental, one person jostling another on a busy pavement. It was easy to rationalize, to believe what he wanted to believe, especially when the alternative was so absurd.

Nevertheless, the Major was circumspect. He drove the Mini to the station with extra care. He stood well back from the edge of the platform as the train came in. He avoided a seat near the door of the carriage, and he inspected his fellow passengers with more than usual interest. He felt a fool.

Luckily this Tuesday he had no business commitments. He had made no arrangement to meet his daughter, Jill, as he sometimes did, and there was no real need to call at the club; he could always phone the porter. He was able to take a taxi directly to the small mews house in Kensington where Jean Aubyn lived.

Letting himself in, he experienced his customary uplift of spirits and, something more, something he would have been ashamed to admit—a feeling of real relief, a feeling that he was safe here, that he need no longer be on his guard.

'Jean,' he called. 'It's me, darling. Are you there?'

He wasn't surprised at the lack of an answer. It was early and Jean wouldn't be expecting him yet. He climbed the stairs, his knee hurting a little, to the studio on the top floor. Sometimes when she was working she became so absorbed that she was unaware of anything, and might not have heard him. But, to his disappointment, she wasn't there. She was out, probably shopping for their dinner; she loved to cook.

He crossed to the window. From here he could see her coming, whichever way she entered the mews. He stood, looking down.

A nondescript grey van was bumping over the cobbles below; it braked at the narrow archway that marked the entrance to the street beyond the mews. A woman was entering, and raised her hand in salutation to the van's driver. It had been nice of him to wait for her to come through the narrow space and not squash her against the wall.

The Major watched her with pleasure. Jean Aubyn, a children's book illustrator, was about fifty, but her tall, athletic figure made her look a lot younger. Short grey hair, lively brown eyes, sunburnt skin, not beautiful — her mouth was too wide, her nose too long and slightly crooked — but most attractive.

It was nearly twenty years, Tom Cheryl thought, since they had first become lovers, and their relationship had matured with time. He hurried down the stairs to greet her. For her part, her heartbeat quickened when she caught sight of him framed in the doorway. Tom. Dear Tom. He was early today, which was splendid. Swinging her shopping basket, she hastened towards him.

The second advertisement appeared two days later, again on Thursday's book page. It was the same size as before, and in the same prime position. And Aileen Cheryl had again folded the paper so that it was the first thing to catch her husband's eye as he sat down to breakfast. There was a difference, however, as the Major realized immediately.

The wording of the ad had changed. Instead of 'Coming Soon — THE DEATH OF MAJOR CHERYL', it read 'Coming Next Tuesday — THE DEATH OF MAJOR CHERYL'. The date — the immediacy — knifed through him. It was almost a challenge. Tuesday! His day for London — Jean's day! For a single incredible moment it crossed his mind that Aileen had inserted the advertisements, that she knew about Jean and was seeking some kind of revenge.

He dismissed the idea as soon as it occurred to him. Aileen had her faults — as he had — but she wasn't in the least devious. Anyway, she must have known for years that he had someone, and she had never cared.

But Tuesday! He'd told Jean about the first advertisement, which she hadn't noticed — she took the newspaper but sometimes never bothered to open it — and about the motor-cyclist and the Oxford incident. Of course she'd been sympathetic, especially when she saw his horribly discoloured knee, but she had agreed it must all be due to coincidence. They'd laughed about it — she'd promised to buy him the book when it appeared — and none of it had seemed important anymore.

The Major heaved a sigh. He wished he could recover that light-heartedness now. But, without Jean, it was no use. He couldn't entirely reassure himself. A specific day had been assigned for the death of Major Cheryl and, however irrational it might seem, he couldn't dissociate himself from it, not after the events of the previous week.

But one thing was for sure, he thought, as he gave Sal the remains of his scrambled eggs, the damned ad wasn't going to stop him going to London as usual on Tuesday. He didn't intend to miss seeing Jean because he was scared. And in the meantime he'd do his best to put a bland face on whatever supposedly funny comments came his way.

'Come on, girl,' he said as the boxer finished licking his plate. 'Walk. But we won't go through the village, and we'll give the pub a miss today. Let the gossips get along without us.'

Tom Cheryl tried his best to follow his usual routine in the days that followed, but in spite of himself he became more edgy and morose as the weekend approached. It wasn't surprising that on Monday night he couldn't sleep.

He lay on his back, hands behind his head, and listened to Sal's steady snoring. He thought of the steps he might have taken to resolve the issue. Get in touch with the newspaper? Try to trace the publishers of the wretched book? Why had he done nothing? Pure bloody-mindedness, he supposed. A refusal to be stampeded into stupid action by a stupid ad. At least the matter would soon be over. Either *The Death of Major Cheryl* would be in the bookshops tomorrow, or—

On this unsatisfactory note he began to relax. It was very quiet and peaceful, as the house was set well back from the road. It was one of the reasons he and Aileen had bought the place. He smiled reminiscently, and drifted into sleep.

He woke with a start, his heart thumping, his pyjamas damp with sweat. He had been dreaming. He wiped his forehead with the back of his hand. For a moment the nightmare had confused him, but as he came fully awake he was convinced that whatever had woken him was real.

He got up and went to the window. He thought he heard the crunch of a footstep on gravel, though there was nothing to be seen in the dark night. Sal hadn't stirred, but she was getting deaf. There could be someone in the garden—a vandal, a burglar, someone looking for a car to steal.

Reluctantly putting on a gown and slippers, he called to the dog. 'Come on, Sal. Walk, girl,' and the magic word woke her. She lumbered after him down the stairs and stood hopefully by the front door while the Major glanced into the downstairs rooms. There was no sign of any attempt at a break-in, and he would have liked to go back to bed and forget the whole thing. But he had promised Sal. He unlocked the front door.

'Out you go, Sal.'

The boxer went willingly, and she didn't bark as she would have done if she sensed the presence of a stranger. Tom Cheryl awaited her return with some impatience. He whistled, but she still didn't appear. A car went by at the end of the drive, and he thought he heard a motorcycle in the distance. And now he could hear Sal in the shrubbery at the side of the house. Obviously she had found something to interest her.

Irritated, he went after her. He hadn't bothered to get a flashlight and in the dark he stumbled against the Mini—in the summer they never put it in the garage. He hit his injured knee and fell heavily against the side of the car. He swore.

'Come here, Sal! At once!'

His voice was sharp and this time the dog obeyed immediately. He patted her on the head. It wasn't her fault he'd fallen. She was a good old bitch, a wonderful companion.

They went back into the house together, and Sal waited while the Major locked up and put out the lights. Upstairs, he was about to go into his bedroom when Aileen flung open the door of her room. She was angry. She too had had difficulty in sleeping, and it was infuriating to be awakened again by Tom's thoughtlessness.

'What on earth have you been up to, Tom?'

'Nothing.' He was taken aback by her aggressiveness.

'Don't be so stupid. You've been outside. I heard you banging about. And look at the state you're in. You're covered with filth. You look as if you've been messing around with the cars. What have you been doing?'

'I'm sorry,' said the Major shortly. 'Obviously I was just taking a stroll in the dark.'

He knew it was an annoying response, but he didn't care. Aileen was in no mood to listen to an explanation. As for the dirt on his dressing-gown, he was as surprised as she; it must have happened when he fell against the Mini. But he wasn't going to tell her about that; she was hardly likely to be in the least sympathetic.

'I'm sorry if I disturbed you,' he added. 'Goodnight, Aileen.'

His wife didn't answer. She went into her room and shut the door. And that might have been the end of the matter, except that the next day Aileen Cheryl happened to mention the incident with some asperity to her friend Mrs Dawlish, and Nina Dawlish remembered.

Tuesday morning. It was raining heavily and Tom Cheryl, tired but determined, made a run for the Mini. As he let the engine idle for a moment, his thoughts were on London. For once he had a busy day ahead before he could go to Jean's — a couple of calls in the City, a present to buy for Aileen's birthday, lunch at his club with his daughter Jill.

He had no intention of driving to London. Aileen was using the Jaguar, and the old Mini was really only suitable for country lanes. It was much more convenient to leave it at the station, just twenty minutes away, and take a fast train.

Today of all days he took special care with his driving. In any case, conditions were poor. The windshield wipers were fighting a losing battle against the increasing downpour, and visibility was limited.

He was now at the top of the steep winding hill that led down to the station. Even in good weather it was wise to treat it with respect. Today it could be slippery with wet leaves. But in five minutes or less he would be parking in the station yard. He breathed a sigh of relief. At the back of his mind had been the thought that the wild motor-cyclist might reappear. He smiled sardonically, admitting his fears.

The next moment Tom Cheryl was seized with panic. The Mini was gathering speed, in spite of his foot on the brake. He pumped it up and down, but there was no response. He pulled on the handbrake. Nothing.

His stomach muscles tight, his mouth dry, the Major gripped the wheel. If he managed to get the Mini to the bottom of the hill in one piece, they would run straight into the wall of the station building, and that would be the end of him, the death of Major . . . There was no way this could be an accident. Someone had tampered with the car. That intruder last night. Tom Cheryl wrenched his thoughts back to the present.

Quickly he switched off the ignition, but he was in top gear and the braking effect of the engine was slight. Try to change down? There was no guarantee he could crash into a lower gear, and he might finish up with even less control. He felt the tail of the Mini hit the bank as they slithered round a slight bend, and then a short level stretch gave him a moment's respite. Suddenly he was able to visualize the road ahead. He had a choice between plunging down the last hill into the station wall and almost certain death, or— He braced himself for the alternative.

As the level stretch was consumed and the road dropped sharply to the right, he made no attempt to take the corner. Instead, he aimed the car straight ahead at a point where there was hedgerow, but no obvious bank. He had no idea what was on the further side. He could only pray there wasn't a ditch that would make the Mini turn turtle. But at least this gave him a chance.

The Mini mounted the slight verge, tore through the hedge, and took off, landing with a shuddering crash in a field two feet below the level of the road. Tom Cheryl lost his grip on the wheel as the Mini bounced. He could see what was coming, for the field sloped steeply down to a thick belt of trees. Suddenly an undulation in the ground slewed the car to the left, and the offside door flew open. With great presence of mind, the Major grabbed at his seat-belt release and threw himself clear. He landed heavily on his side and watched, half stunned, as the car plunged downwards. As it hit the trees it overturned, and a flame flickered when petrol from the tank found the hot engine.

CHAPTER 3

Of the three people who expected to meet Major Cheryl that morning only one was seriously upset when he failed to keep his appointments. The Chairman of the Board delayed the Directors' Meeting a mere five minutes because of his absence, and then proceeded with the agenda; it was unusual but not unknown for non-executive directors like the Major to be absent without previous apology. His stockbroker waited longer and was more irritated, but soon forgot about him when another client arrived. Jill Cheryl alone was worried. Her father had never before stood her up like this.

The Major had arranged to meet her at his club at twelve-thirty. She was punctual, but expected him to be there already. When the porter said he hadn't yet arrived she read the announcements on the notice boards, studied the news being extruded by the teleprinter, sat down, stood up, inspected the huge oil painting that dominated the hall until she could have described it in detail, and finally returned to the porter. It was after one o'clock.

'You're sure my father hasn't telephoned?'

It wasn't an unreasonable question, as the phone at the porter's desk had been ringing incessantly. 'I'm afraid not, miss.' The porter smiled his sympathy. She was an attractive girl and he liked her. He wished he could help.

'And you're certain he's not in the club?'

'Positive, miss,' said the porter. 'I've been on duty since nine and Major Cheryl's not been in today. In any case,' he added, not unreasonably, 'if he was in the building he'd have been down to meet you by now.'

'Thank you. You're quite right,' said Jill.

'If you'd care to use the phone, miss.' The porter pointed to the row of call-boxes.

Jill Cheryl hesitated. It was unlikely there would be anyone at home, but she could call Jean Aubyn. Conceivably her father had forgotten his date with her and gone straight to Jean's. At least it was worth a try.

But Jean denied all knowledge of his movements. 'No, Jill. I haven't seen or heard from him today. He said he wouldn't be here till tea-time. He made a point of telling me because—' Her voice trailed away. 'Christ!'

'What is it? What's the matter?'

'The ads in the paper. The last one—'

'What ads? What paper?' Jill was impatient. She liked Jean, even admired her, and understood her relationship with Tom, but she could be irritatingly vague on occasion. 'I don't know what you're talking about.'

'Have you phoned Farlingham?'

'No. Mother's sure to be out, and if Dad's there he'd have—'

'Jill, please, listen! Do as I ask. If you can find out what—what's going on, what's delaying him, call me back. If not, come round here right away. I'll give you some lunch. Come anyway. Please!'

Jean tried to quell her rising fear as she put down the receiver. If anything had happened to Tom . . . But why should it? Probably he'd been kept at a meeting, or was unable to get a taxi or—something. She willed the phone to ring, for Jill to call with a simple explanation. It was frustrating not to be able to be directly involved, to be always at one remove from the man she loved. Maybe she and Tom should have taken the plunge into divorces twenty years ago, in spite of his small children and her husband's paralysis. But they hadn't, and she could only wait for news.

The telephone remained obstinately silent, and she went to the window and stood staring down into the mews. That wretched grey van was still parked opposite, and the sight of it annoyed her again. It had been there most of the morning, and she'd seen it on other occasions. Once she'd reported its number to the police for obstructing the mews. They'd done nothing, as usual. She thought of going down and telling the man, whom she could only see as a shadow behind the wheel, that parking was forbidden there. But at that moment Jill arrived.

'As I expected, no answer from Farlingham,' Jill said at once as Jean opened the door. 'So at any rate Dad's not ill.'

'It might be better if—' Jean began, and checked herself. 'No. I'm being a fool. Come in, Jill, and we'll have some lunch and I'll show you those bloody ads. You say Tom never told you about them?'

'I've not seen him for several weeks. I've been in Italy on holiday. I went—'

Mutual explanations followed. Jill's initial reaction to the story was one of amusement. The ads were clearly promotions for a book, teasers for a thriller. It was chance that the author had named his character 'Major Cheryl'.

The motor-cyclist could be put down to coincidence, and the bus incident to a misunderstanding or her father's imagination.

Nevertheless, Jean's acute anxiety was obvious and infectious, and Jill spent the afternoon trying to phone her parents' home, but without success. Neither had the Major's club heard from him. The two women were reluctant to make more extensive enquiries, at least until a few more hours had passed. In any case, they were uncertain how to set about effective queries without introducing incredible complications. The police? Tell the whole tale from the beginning? The mind boggled, especially as the Major might reappear at any time. Jean tried to work in her studio. Jill spent the time by the phone, hoping against hope that her father would call.

Finally, about six o'clock, after dialling her home number once again, Jill heard her mother's answering voice. She didn't bother with pleasantries.

'Mother, do you know where Dad is? Is he all right? I was meant to be meeting him for lunch but—'

To Jean, pacing the room, there followed a seemingly endless monologue. Jill listened, nodding at intervals. At last, she said, 'Okay, Mother, I'll come down tomorrow. Goodbye till then.' She put down the receiver.

'Is he—? Is he—?' Jean was unable to contain herself, but she couldn't frame the question.

'No!' Jill said quickly. 'He's had an accident, but he's not even badly hurt.'

'Thank God for that.' Jean Aubyn went to a side table that held an array of bottles, poured herself an inch of whisky and drank it neat. She held the bottle and a glass out to Jill. She was trembling. 'What happened?'

Jill eyed her with sympathy. 'It's all right,' she repeated quickly. 'He's not hurt. According to Mother, his brakes failed when he was going down the station hill this morning in the Mini. It was raining and the road was slippery. The car went off the road and across a field. Dad was thrown clear and he's just mildly shocked and concussed. They took him to Oxford for X-rays, but they expect to let him out of hospital in a day or two. He was incredibly lucky, though. The Mini hit some trees and burst into flames.'

'I see,' said Jean hesitantly.

'You don't believe it was an accident?'

'No. I don't think I do. The coincidence is too great. It doesn't make sense.'

Jill hesitated, considering. She said slowly, 'It doesn't make sense that anyone should want to kill Dad, either. And why warn him in advance, even name the day?'

'I don't know,' Jean said, 'but I'm afraid, horribly afraid.'

CHAPTER 4

After three days of poor weather, Friday was fine and clear and sunny. Tom Cheryl sat in his garden, a magazine open on his lap. He wasn't reading. He watched some wood-pigeons pecking at the grain he'd thrown down for them, and noticed that the grass needed mowing. He tried to make his mind a blank. He was tired of thinking, wondering, puzzling, getting nowhere.

He had been discharged from the hospital yesterday. Jill had fetched him in the morning. He was to rest, take things easily for a few days, but he was fine. The doctors had been most reassuring. There was nothing for him to worry about.

Nothing to worry about! Tom Cheryl gritted his teeth. For some reason newspaper deliveries in the hospital had been delayed yesterday, but Jill had a copy of the important one in the car for him, open at the book page.

He had no idea what he expected to find. Yet, after one glance at the advertisement, in the same double-column style and at the top of the same right-hand page, he knew he could have foreseen it. *'Postponed'*, it read, *'but Coming Soon* — THE DEATH OF MAJOR CHERYL'.

A sound disturbed his unhappy thoughts, and the Major looked up. His wife had come out on the terrace and behind her, framed in the french windows, was the Reverend Edwin Galverstone.

'Tom, here's the vicar come to see you.' Aileen stood, self-possessed and purposeful as always, smiling from one man to the other. 'I'm just off. It's my "Meals on Wheels" day, remember. Will you be all right? Jill should be home soon.'

'We'll be fine,' the vicar interposed before Tom Cheryl could speak. 'Don't you worry, my dear. You get along to your good works. I'll look after him.'

'I don't need looking after, Edwin, thank you all the same,' the Major said coldly as Aileen left them. 'There's nothing wrong with me.'

'Good! Splendid!' Galverstone stretched himself out on a deck-chair and gave a wry, somewhat apologetic smile. 'I'm afraid Aileen always makes me sound more — more unctuous than I really am, Tom, and she did say you were a bit fraught. Not surprising in the circumstances.'

The Major restrained the sharp retort that sprang to his lips, and silently cursed his wife. For a moment he hesitated, wondering whether to take Edwin Galverstone fully into his confidence. But there was so little to tell — suspicions, doubts, damn all else — and nothing Edwin could do about them.

'Tom, these peculiar notices in the newspaper,' the vicar continued. 'The first one was something of a joke, but the others — they've been so singularly apt. You could have been killed on Tuesday, but you weren't. Yet the threat — if it is a threat — remains, as far as I can see. Bill

Marshall says you could probably sue the paper, or —'

'Bill Marshall? What the hell's it got to do with him?
He's not my solicitor. I haven't asked him for advice. If I
wanted any I certainly wouldn't go to him.'

'No. Quite. Quite.' Edwin Galverstone made a steeple
of his hands. 'But he wasn't speaking professionally,
Tom. He was just —'

'Just what? Gossiping? Tell him to mind his own
business. It's nothing to do with him, or anyone else.'

'People talk, Tom. You can't stop them, especially in a
small place like this. And you must admit they've got
some justification. You'd talk yourself if you heard of
anyone else in this sort of strange situation.'

The Major didn't reply. Edwin was right, of course.
You couldn't stop people talking. That didn't mean it was
pleasant to be the subject of their sniggering gossip, to be
made to feel a fool through no fault of one's own — and, at
the same time, to have a cold nub of fear inside. A
strange situation? It was bizarre. It was surreal, though
he'd never been quite sure what the word meant.

'What have the police had to say?'

'What?' The Major hadn't been listening.

'The police. When you told them about the
advertisements?'

'I didn't need to tell them. They'd noticed them
already,' the Major said testily. 'I expect it was that
damned doctor — Carson, you know — who mentioned
them. He called yesterday and hinted that I might have
put them in the paper myself! I still don't know if the little
man was serious or not. Anyway, the police weren't that
interested in the ads. It was the car crash they were fussing
about. And even then there was only one person involved
and no serious damage, except to my own car. I told them
my brakes had failed, but they put it down to a fault or poor
maintenance or something. The car's burnt out, and there's
no way they can tell for sure what happened.'

'But didn't they think the accident was more than just a coincidence? At least they could do some checking with the newspaper.'

'Why should they? Coincidences are always happening. Million to one shots. They probably think the ads made me expect to have some sort of crash, so I brought it on myself.'

Tom Cheryl heard the bitterness in his voice, and regretted it. Edwin was watching him with a worried, dubious expression. He shouldn't have made that crack about the police. It was true they hadn't been exactly sympathetic when they saw him in hospital. It was pure routine as far as they were concerned. Perhaps that was why he hadn't mentioned the intruder he thought he'd heard in the garden on Monday night. Aileen had been at his bedside at the time, and he'd waited for her to prompt him, but she hadn't, and the moment had passed. He sighed.

'Edwin, I'm sorry, but I don't want to discuss it anymore.' The Major stood up and the vicar felt bound to do the same. 'And I'd be grateful if you tried to discourage talk in the village.'

'Yes, of course. I'll do my best. I always do.'

If Tom Cheryl noticed the slight reproof in Edwin Galverstone's last words, he didn't show it, and a possibly embarrassing moment was avoided by the sound of the phone in the house and the arrival of the boxer on the terrace. The ringing stopped, and Sal came quickly to her master.

'Hello, girl.' He patted her on the head. 'Jill must be back. She was taking Sal for a walk. She'll make us some coffee, if you'd like a cup, Edwin.' It was a peace offering.

'Thanks, but no. I must be off, Tom.'

The two men chatted amicably about their gardens, and then the vicar left, feeling he had been of little use and half regretting his visit. Tom Cheryl heaved another sigh, this time of relief; he was thankful to be alone. He didn't count Jill. He was very fond of both the girls, but Jill had always been his favourite. He wished she'd marry and have children. He and Aileen weren't much of an example of wedded bliss, but Celia had married happily, and if one sister, why not the other?

Jill would have been surprised at his thoughts, and a little touched. She caught herself frowning fiercely as she carried out the coffee tray. Her father had a lot to worry about at the moment, and the bloody business was getting her down too.

'Here we are, Dad,' she said, trying to sound cheerful. 'Coffee. And some chocolate biscuits. I'm glad the Rev's gone, because I've got some news for you.'

'Good news?'

'I wouldn't say that, exactly, but —' She shrugged. 'Jean phoned just as I came in. According to her publishing friends, the ads for "The Death of Major C" haven't caused wild interest in the trade. They say that sort of promotion's been tried before many times. Publishers are notoriously an ingrown lot, only interested in their own books, but there's been a little talk. For example, one would expect a few proof copies to be around, and they're not, so it's been suggested the ads might be a hoax of some kind. But the paper denies this, though it's keeping very mum. Someone in its advertising department claims that a very reputable publishing house is paying good money to have them inserted.'

'Which leaves us just where we came in. Damn!' The Major swore. 'I was pinning a good deal on Jean. I was hoping she could track down some sort of lead, though God knows what to. But if it's odds on the ads are genuine . . .' He shook his head glumly, then brightened. 'Not that it's all that important, I suppose. Apart from the demise of the old Mini, there's been no real damage yet. You know, it's one of the odd things about this joker, if there is one. He's gone to an awful lot of trouble without much to show for it.'

On Sunday morning the Major refused to face church with his wife and daughter. Too much gossip, he said. Instead, he'd take Sal for her walk. He waited until the women had left and then called the boxer.

Together they left the drive and turned away from the church. They followed their normal route, through lanes and field paths, the dog running ahead or lingering behind the Major, but never far away. Eventually, after about half an hour, they emerged on to a minor road — an obvious choice for a direct return to the village. Sometimes there was fast local traffic on this road, and the Major, ever careful, put Sal on her lead again.

There was a sudden deafening roar behind them. The Major turned sharply. He couldn't be said to recognize the yellow-helmeted, black-garbed figure hurtling towards him on a motor-bike, but instinct told him that this was the enemy.

Tom Cheryl leapt for the hedge, hauling at Sal's lead. Unwittingly, she hampered him, and he tripped, sprawling in the ditch, conscious of a confusion of sounds, the thunder of the bike as it swerved away from him at the last moment, and a high, thin howl from Sal.

After the heavy rain earlier in the week the ditch was full of muddy water. Tom Cheryl got up slowly, first on to his knees, then to his feet. He was filthy, plastered with mud and grass, with bits of twig in his hair. He didn't improve his appearance by running his hands over his head in an effort to remove them. He was shaken, but otherwise unhurt. Automatically he began to brush down his clothes, hardly aware of his actions, his mind concentrated on cursing the unknown man who had caused the incident.

By now the noise of the motor-cycle had disappeared

into the distance. But the lonely road was no place to linger. He didn't want to be attacked again. The sooner they got home, the better. He looked round for the boxer.

'Sal! Sal! Where are you? Come here, girl!'

There was no response, and the Major frowned. Where was Sal? He called again, more loudly, but still the dog didn't answer. He heard a car approaching, travelling fast, and he drew well into the side, prepared to jump if necessary. But it was only a family party, father, mother, children, probably on their way to Sunday lunch. The woman stared at him as they passed, and the Major saw her say something to her husband. They didn't stop, but the children watched him, their noses pressed against the rear window, until the car turned a corner.

The Major didn't blame them. He knew he must look a curious sight. He glanced down at himself, and at that moment saw Sal.

The boxer was lying in the ditch. She was on her back, half-submerged in the muddy water. She was clearly dead, her head lolling at an impossible angle, though her eyes were open, pleading.

Tom Cheryl choked on his emotions. Falling to his knees, he plunged his arms into the mud and filth, and heaved the dog's body on to the road. It wasn't easy. She was heavy, and the angle of lift was all wrong, but he managed somehow.

He got to his feet and looked about him. He couldn't let Sal lie like this in the open, but it was pointless to try to carry her. He spotted a thinning in the hedge, forced his way through and found a place to leave her. Then he set off for home.

His thoughts were chaotic, but his immediate objective was to get the car, collect Sal's body and bury it decently in his garden. He forgot the time. He forgot it was Sunday. He forgot his own appearance. He was seething with anger that his dog should have been killed brutally and to no apparent purpose. He took the shortest way back to the house. Unfortunately, it happened to be through the churchyard.

It was a little after twelve when he came round the corner of the old Norman church. The Reverend Edwin Galverstone had dismissed the congregation some five minutes ago, and was standing in the porch shaking hands as his parishioners filed out. Some were lingering to chat. With the summer visitors added to the locals it was quite a large gathering.

Tom Cheryl's sudden appearance, grim and purposeful, his face scratched and filthy, his clothes mud-covered, caused a frisson of apprehension to run through the assembly. Conversations tailed away. Everyone turned to stare. Even the strangers, spending but a few days in Farlingham, were intrigued.

Jill was the first to reach her father. 'Dad, what is it? What's happened? Are you all right?'

Tom Cheryl, taken aback by the crowd of people surrounding him, answered without thinking.

'The bugger's killed Sal,' he said, his voice loud with anger.

'Thomas! Really!' Whereas Jill was anxious, Aileen Cheryl was furious. 'How dare you use such language in front of the vicar and—and everyone. You should be ashamed. And look at you. What have you been doing? Your suit's ruined—and your beautiful watch.'

Even the Major realized that his wife's response was not entirely rational, was a mere first reaction to his sudden appearance in such unexpected circumstances, but he himself was too angry to care for the proprieties.

'Damn my suit! And my watch! Didn't you hear what I said, Aileen? Sal's dead. I had to leave her. She was too heavy to carry. I must get the car and fetch her.'

'What in? Not my car! I'm not having a dead dog messing up the Jaguar!'

Such stupid anger was unlike Aileen. She prided herself on being calm and civilized, whatever the provocation. But Tom had embarrassed her in front of friends and acquaintances, and she could imagine the story of this Sunday morning being repeated and embellished.

Nor was this a moment when Tom Cheryl could be forbearing. He looked at his wife as if she were a stranger. Her reference to Sal as 'a dead dog' had shocked him. He lifted his arm.

But Edwin Galverstone had thrust his way between them. 'We'll take my car, Tom. It's right here. It'll save you going home. There's a rug in the back that'll do nicely to wrap poor Sal in.'

The sympathetic gesture calmed Tom, and with the vicar on one side and Jill on the other he allowed himself to be led away. Aileen was left to the commiserations of Nina Dawlish and various friends. Later, they were to swear that, if the vicar hadn't intervened, Major Cheryl would have struck his wife.

CHAPTER 5

On Tuesday Major Cheryl went to London as usual. His wife tried to dissuade him, but not very hard. In any case, he was determined. It was two weeks since he had seen Jean, though he had phoned her once or twice when Aileen was out. What was more, he had an appointment at New Scotland Yard.

Sal's death—he thought of it as a barbaric act of murder—had finally persuaded him to tackle the police again, as Edwin and Jill had been urging. Aileen's attitude had been more ambiguous. She regretted her outburst on Sunday morning, but she still found herself unable to take at all seriously the advertisements and the incidents that seemed to accompany them.

Though he acknowledged the need to consult the authorities, the Major was adamant that the locals would be of little help. He would go to the top, or nowhere. Accordingly, he had spent Monday tracking down an ex-army acquaintance, now a politician with influence in the Home Office, to whom he told a little of his story, and who had been able to arrange an appointment with a CID Chief Superintendent in London.

Jill insisted on driving her father to town. She said it would probably be her only chance to see the inside of the Yard, and she wasn't going to miss it. In fact, she was becoming more and more concerned, and she didn't intend to let the Major out of her sight until he was safe in Jean Aubyn's house for the night.

They lunched with Jean, and in the afternoon took a taxi to the modern office block on Victoria Street that was now the headquarters of the Metropolitan Police. Even this change made the Major slightly uneasy. He remembered nostalgically his days at the Ministry of Defence, almost next door to the old Scotland Yard buildings on the Embankment.

They were expected at the Yard, and a young Constable escorted them from the entrance hall to the office of a Detective Chief Superintendent Harris. It was a big, bright room, efficient rather than comfortable, and the Chief Superintendent came forward to greet them from behind a large grey steel desk.

'Good afternoon, Major Cheryl,' he said, holding out his hand. 'I've been told you've got a rather interesting story for me.' He looked enquiringly at Jill.

'This is my daughter, Chief Superintendent,' the Major said. 'She drove me up to town today, and she may be able to add something to the tale.'

'I see,' said the Chief Superintendent. 'Good afternoon, Miss Cheryl. You're very welcome. Now may I introduce

Detective Chief Inspector Taylor?'

The Chief Inspector was standing by the window, gazing down into the busy street below. He turned and bowed politely as the visitors were seated, but didn't offer to shake hands. He seemed a little preoccupied, as indeed he was. He had plenty on his plate at the moment, and had no particular wish to be dragged in to this interview. As far as he could see, from what his Chief had said, it was a funny affair, a case that would probably turn out not to be a case at all. He eyed the Major and his daughter with some curiosity. Cheryl he could place instantly—a typical retired service officer. The daughter was another matter. Moderate height, light brown hair, pleasant features with a determined jaw, good figure; in all, a most attractive woman, and probably holding down some responsible job. His thoughts were interrupted by the arrival of a Constable with a tea tray. The Chief Superintendent stood up.

'Major Cheryl, I know you're going to think me very rude, but an unexpected meeting's come up. I can't possibly cut it, much as I'd like to. Chief Inspector Taylor here will do anything he can to help you, and he'll report to me. But I must warn you, Major, that this is all slightly irregular. I understand you have reasons for not wanting to approach your local police—the Thames Valley force—but I'm sure you understand that what you say here could make it necessary for us to contact them.'

This was fairly intimidating, but even if the Major had wanted to reply or protest or explain, he had no chance. The Chief Superintendent was already at the door and the Chief Inspector was seating himself behind the desk, reaching for the tea tray.

'Milk and sugar, Miss Cheryl?'

The Major took a long breath and expelled it slowly. On reflection he couldn't help admiring the neat way in which he had been passed on to the junior man, but it depressed him. He was, as he had half-expected, about to waste his time. Nothing would come of this visit to the CID—except perhaps local complications. And, in this belief, as soon as the tea-pouring ceremony was over, he told his story baldly, as if he scarcely credited it himself.

Jill, wishing her father wouldn't sound quite so detached, so—so unsympathetic, watched the Chief Inspector carefully, but learned little from his reactions. He seemed to listen with interest. He made the occasional note, asked the occasional question. But it was impossible to guess what he was thinking; his face gave nothing away.

It was an attractive face, Jill thought, lean, with a good bone structure and, surprisingly since his hair was almost black, blue eyes. He would be in his late thirties, perhaps, ambitious and, to judge from his well-tailored suit, doing very nicely for himself. But he was married; he wore a wedding ring. She flushed as he suddenly glanced up and their eyes met. She wished he wouldn't read her thoughts.

'And that's all you can tell me, sir?' Chief Inspector Taylor said, returning his gaze to Tom Cheryl.

'Yes. I know you must think it's all a lot of nonsense, but—'

'Not at all, sir,' Taylor said politely. 'But at this stage I can't do more than repeat the Chief Superintendent's comment. You know how we work at the Yard. We can only intervene in purely local affairs if we're formally called in. But clearly there could well be London angles here, which would give us an excuse to take some action. Anyway, I'll report to my superiors, and you can be assured we'll do everything we can to put an end to this—this unpleasant business. If we do contact Kidlington—that's the Headquarters of the Thames Valley boys—we'll be most discreet.' Just perceptibly he pushed back his chair to indicate that the interview was at an end. 'I'll be in touch if I've anything to report, sir,' he added. His smile included them both.

Neither of them returned the smile. The Major nodded and stood up. As far as he was concerned the afternoon would have been more rewardingly spent with his stockbroker or, better still, with Jean. Jill also stood. She understood her father's disappointment. Obviously nothing of any value had been achieved. Irrationally she blamed the policeman.

She said icily, 'I'm sure you'll do your best, Chief Inspector. I only hope it'll be good enough—before something worse happens to my father.'

'Indeed, I hope so too, Miss Cheryl,' he replied. He wished he could have been more helpful, if only because she seemed such a pleasant and determined girl, but he sensed that anything more than a formal response would infuriate her. 'I'll give the matter my immediate attention, I promise.'

But there was really very little he could do, David Taylor thought as he returned to his office after seeing the Cheryls down to the entrance hall. Check on the advertisements, yes. The threats, if they were real threats, seemed to originate in London, but all the alleged attacks on Major Cheryl had taken place in Oxfordshire, outside his jurisdiction. He would have to get the Chief Superintendent to clear things with the locals before he started anything there. And what was there to start? The car crash—the only event that had left any really concrete evidence—had apparently already been investigated.

And why had the Major been so reluctant to approach his local police directly? He said he thought they were unlikely to take him seriously, but he was a well-known figure in his own area. Surely he could have tackled the matter at a high enough level to get a reasonable hearing. If anything, the Yard was likely to be more, rather than less, sceptical. Certainly, it had enough work of its own without wasting time and taxpayers' money on what was probably no more than an unpleasant hoax. He sighed. Anyway, it was too late to take any action tonight. Tomorrow would be another day. He'd have to put on some sort of show, if only to please his Chief—and Miss Cheryl. Her father had called her Jill. The name suited her. Nice girl. He smiled reminiscently.

'Now, tread carefully, Brian.' The next morning David Taylor was in his office briefing Detective-Sergeant Drew. 'I'd rather like to go myself, but I've got to be in court. You know what newspaper editors are like over questions of this kind. I've told you as much as I know about the affair, but don't let them get a hint that there might be a story in it. Just say it's a routine enquiry, and we'd be most grateful if they'd lend us a hand and tell us which publishers inserted those ads. Hint at favours to come, if you have to, but don't go too far.'

'All right, sir. I understand.' Drew was ten years older than David Taylor, competent, efficient, but with a dislike for the greater responsibility that would come with an Inspector's rank. The two of them had worked together before, and they got on well. 'What about the Farlingham end?' Drew added.

'I've had a word with the Chief. He thinks it's all right for us to look into the London angles before we approach the locals. After all, if we can sort out these wretched ads, there may be no more to it. Let's see what the form is here, before we rock any boats. Okay?'

Fortunately, for once the Chief Inspector was not kept waiting at the court, and his appearance was brief. He was back at his desk when Drew returned from Fleet Street.

'I'm afraid it was as you guessed, sir. They're playing it very cool. The first thing they asked was if anything criminal was involved. If not, it might be a matter of civil libel. In either case, they'd want to consult their lawyers before saying anything. I thought of what you'd said, and I didn't claim any urgency. What I did do was make an appointment for you to see the Managing Editor at five this evening. That's what they seemed to want, and I hope it's all right.'

'That's fine. I think I'll go alone; it'll look less formal. I'll tell them a bit of the story, and see if I can't persuade them to budge without involving lawyers at this stage.'

In fact, David Taylor found the Managing Editor more amenable than he had expected. The Chief Inspector gave a brief explanation of the situation, admitting that there seemed to be some connection between these anonymous advertisements and a number of trivial incidents affecting a real Major. The editor, a cheerful character in his shirt-sleeves, had been looking into the matter during the afternoon, and had assured himself that his paper had done no more than act strictly in accordance with its instructions. He was fully prepared to produce the original letter and the advertisement copy.

David Taylor scanned the papers with interest— Lindsay & Beckett letterhead, apparently professionally typed—though it was hard to tell with an electric machine, which this certainly was—seemingly signed by one of the firm's directors, addressed to the paper's advertisement manager:

Dear Sir,

We should be grateful if you would set and publish the enclosed display advertisements in 10 cm double-column plain-bordered boxes on your book pages, on Thursday . . . and each succeeding Thursday, in their numbered sequence. When publication is complete, please bill Lindsay & Beckett, as above. In view of the 'teasing' nature of these announcements, we should be glad if you would not respond to any enquiries as to their origin until further notice. As you will see the copy is extremely simple, and we do not require to see proofs.

Yours truly,
James Lindsay,
Director.

'You can see why we weren't too anxious to cooperate with your Sergeant,' said the editor, pointing to the sentence about secrecy. 'Campaigns of this kind aren't that unusual in the book business, though they're more usual in the trade press than in general newspapers.'

David Taylor was studying the advertising copy. Three of the ads he had seen in print. The fourth, due for publication tomorrow, read: '*Final Announcement. Early Next Month* — THE DEATH OF MAJOR CHERYL'.

Early next month, he thought — the first will be next Tuesday. Aloud, he said, 'Is this the usual form for an order of this kind?'

'Well, advertisers vary,' said the editor. 'Agencies have their own insertion order forms, and some publishers use forms of the same kind. But you know what publishers' publicity departments are like — or perhaps you don't. Anyway, they're often one man and a dog, and it's by no means unusual for copy to come in like that with an ordinary letter. As long as we know the firm, we accept it without question, especially when there's no artwork involved.'

'And you know Lindsay & Beckett?'

'Of course. Most reputable. You must have heard of them. A good fiction list, including crime novels, they tell me, and some outstanding non-fiction. They advertise with us all the time, though usually in a more — more, what shall I say? — staid fashion.'

'Have you been in touch with Lindsay & Beckett this afternoon?'

'No. I saw no reason to make them think we were questioning their instructions. We've had no reaction to the other ads, and no suggestion of a hoax of any kind. We could check with them, but I expect their offices will be shut by now.'

'And what about this fourth advertisement — this "Final Announcement"?'

'The last in the series — well, those pages are already plated for tomorrow's paper. I think I'd need a court order not to print the ad. As I say, it's the last, and its cancellation could spoil everything for them.'

'I see your point,' said Taylor. 'Frankly, I don't know what to suggest. But I do know there's no way I can get an order for you to change your paper. In any case, it may well be a good thing to print it and see what happens. I'll go to the publishers myself in the morning, and I'd be grateful for photocopies of those papers to take with me. I promise I won't produce them if it's clear there's nothing amiss. But make sure you keep the originals in case we need them.'

'That's all right,' said the editor. He pressed a button by his phone and gave the papers to a secretary with instructions. 'Glad to help. And keep us informed if there's a story in this. "Cheryl" — it's an unusual name. Maybe we should do a little investigating ourselves.'

'I hope you won't,' said the Chief Inspector.

The editor laughed. 'I was only joking,' he said. 'We've got enough to do without trying to prove we've been the victim of a practical joke. Here are your documents,' he added as the secretary reappeared. 'Now, if that's all, I've a paper to get out.'

The fourth advertisement duly appeared the next morning, and David Taylor made a few enquiries of his own before he left the Yard. Lindsay & Beckett weren't the largest publishing house in Britain but, as the editor said, they had an excellent reputation. Their offices were in a tall, narrow building in a Bloomsbury square, its entrance hall a seeming confusion of parcels and cartons. A slightly acid receptionist was trying to create some kind of order from this apparent chaos.

'You've got an appointment, you say? With Mr Beckett?' She seemed unimpressed by his Warrant Card. 'There's a gentleman called Taylor here to see you,' she said into a phone. Then to Taylor, 'Go right up. It's the front room on the second floor. Right above this hall.'

Ralph Beckett, a youngish brown-haired man in a neat business suit, looked more like a successful accountant than a publisher, and his book-lined room with its long windows overlooking the square was an oasis of calm. 'What can I do for Scotland Yard?' he said pleasantly.

David said, 'The first thing is to answer one question. Are you about to publish a book called *The Death of Major Cheryl*?'

'Oh,' said Beckett. 'Those ads. No. Certainly not. It's not on our list.'

David paused for a moment and then said, 'In that case, I'd like you to look at these papers. They're only photocopies, but the originals are readily available. In fact, they're in the hands of the paper that's been printing the advertisements.'

Beckett glanced through the letter and the advertising copy. 'It's our letterhead, all right,' he said, 'and it looks like James Lindsay's signature. He's in the States till Monday. But I'm absolutely certain we've nothing of this kind on the boil.' He looked curiously at David. 'And what is this? Where do Scotland Yard come in?'

David hesitated. 'There is a real Major Cheryl,' he said, 'and various unpleasant things seem to be happening to him.'

Beckett laughed. 'You mean the book's coming true before it's published. I've heard of "faction", but this is ridiculous. Look, do you mind if we get James's editorial assistant in—she's a girl called Gladys Lee, and she should know about this too.'

He spoke into a phone, and a few moments later there was a knock at the door.

'Come in, Gladys,' said Beckett. 'This is Detective Chief Inspector Taylor from Scotland Yard. I know you've edited lots of crime stories, but I bet this is the first time you've seen a real CID man in the flesh.'

'Not quite, Ralph,' said Gladys Lee. 'I heard one speak at a Crime Writers' Association meeting. But I've never been so close to one before.'

She was a large girl, overweight, with soft brown eyes behind thick spectacles, and mousy hair. She was wearing a shapeless cardigan over a summer dress, both in an ageing shade of puce that would have flattered no one. She sat down, twiddling a ring on her engagement finger. It wasn't a diamond, Taylor noticed, but gold and turquoise. David Taylor wondered what any man saw in her.

But she was no fool. She studied the papers carefully, and answered the Chief Inspector's questions readily. She had seen the ads for the book, but was sure they were nothing to do with Lindsay & Beckett. The letter was on their headed paper, but she didn't think it had been typed on any of their office machines. These were all electric, and some months ago it had been decided to standardize them and their typefaces.

The signature seemed to be Mr Lindsay's, but it would be unheard of for him to send such an insertion order direct to a newspaper; anything of this kind would go through the publicity department. Apart from this, she could throw no light on the affair. Yes, she could produce a sample of Mr Lindsay's signature, and samples from the office typewriters.

'We keep a record of incoming manuscripts, of course,' added Beckett. 'Get someone to start looking for a title like this over the past—' He looked at Taylor.

Taylor hesitated. 'Four or five years should be quite enough at this stage, I think,' he said.

'Fine,' said Beckett. 'That may take a little time, but I've a good memory, and the name "Cheryl" would probably stick. I'm pretty certain we won't find anything. And, as I say, I know for sure we've never accepted such a book. You agree, Gladys?'

The girl nodded as she left the room, and Beckett turned to Taylor. 'Well, that seems to be that,' he said. 'There's nothing more we can do, is there?'

'No, I suppose not,' said Taylor slowly. 'We'll have to await developments. It's possible that nothing more may come of the matter, though I ought to see Mr Lindsay when he returns. On the other hand, we may have to go into things more thoroughly — proper interviews with your staff, and statements, and so on. I'll be in touch as soon as I can. Thank you,' he added to Gladys Lee, who had returned to hand him a folder.

It was on that note that Taylor left, vaguely dissatisfied. It was becoming quite clear that the advertisements were not genuine, but he remained uncertain what further action might be taken. At least, he thought, he could put the whole thing to the Chief.

CHAPTER 6

The appearance of the 'Final Announcement' of *The Death of Major Cheryl* in Thursday's paper merely added to the tensions of those involved. In Farlingham, Tom Cheryl was in a dour mood. Over the weekend, in spite of protestations from Jill and Edwin Galverstone, he insisted on taking long, solitary walks, though he didn't enjoy them without Sal's company. Jill became increasingly worried about him. Even Aileen was perturbed. She complained to her friend Nina Dawlish that Tom was behaving very strangely these days. The Major's was not a happy household.

Jean Aubyn, biting her nails in London, tried to reassure herself with the thought that before next month, next Tuesday, the police would have put a stop to the whole ridiculous—or terrifying—business. In fact, the police were nowhere near achieving this objective.

David Taylor had reported the outcome of his enquiries to his Chief Superintendent. There was so little to go on that they had decided to play a waiting game, apart from a routine request to the Thames Valley Police for any information about Major Cheryl, and a copy of their report on his crash in his Mini.

The Chief Inspector spent most of Friday in court, and worked long hours in his office on the Saturday and Sunday, returning to his bachelor flat in Dolphin Square quite near the Yard only to sleep. Nevertheless, his in-tray was still piled high on Monday morning, and when the phone announced that a Jill Cheryl was downstairs wanting to see him, he nearly made an excuse. Then he changed his mind.

'Okay. Bring her up.'

It was too late for coffee, but this time he went forward to shake hands. He waved her to a chair. He noticed the elegance of her legs as she sat, and retreated behind his desk.

'How nice to see you, Miss Cheryl. Your father's all right, I know.'

'At the moment, yes. But tomorrow's the first of the month, and we've heard nothing from you.'

'No. I'm sorry, but that's because there's been nothing to report. It's only in the last hour been finally confirmed that the advertisements for this so-called book aren't genuine. Mr Lindsay, the publisher whose firm was supposed to have inserted them, flew back from the States this morning. He denies all knowledge of the letter he's supposed to have signed, and he's questioning his staff right now.'

'You think one of them's responsible for all this?'

'For what an opinion's worth, no, I don't. It would be much too obvious. But it's someone who had access to the firm's stationery and knew Lindsay's signature or got a copy of it. I've a list of the staff here. Perhaps you'd ask your father to look through it and make sure he's never heard of any of the names.'

'Yes, of course.' Jill spoke absently. Suddenly she was genuinely frightened. If the advertisements were spurious, someone purposeful and resourceful really was threatening her father. It was clearly no local individual with some kind of grudge, who might have seen the ads or heard of them in the pub, and taken advantage of the situation. She glanced up and saw the Chief Inspector looking at her anxiously. 'Sorry,' she said, though she didn't know why she was apologizing. 'I'm very fond of Dad. He's a good man. It would be dreadful if anything were to happen to him.'

'Yes, I know.' David Taylor's voice was gentle. 'The difficulty is, it's all so nebulous. If you discount a minor forgery, no real crime's been committed.'

Jill stared at him in surprise. 'What about tampering with the Mini?'

'You know the car was burnt out, Miss Cheryl. There's no evidence. I've just been reading the local police report. There's just no way of telling whether the car was tampered with or not.' He shrugged. 'As for the motor-cyclist your father mentioned, we're not very likely to trace him.'

'Have you tried?'

'No, Miss Cheryl, we have neither the men nor the time to chase will-o'-the-wisps.'

'You mean you're just going to wait till someone kills

my father. That would be evidence.'

'What do you suggest? That we put him under round-the-clock surveillance? In the first place, I'm not sure he'd agree to it, and in the second it isn't practical.' David Taylor restrained his temper. It wasn't the girl's fault that he was tired and over-worked. 'Look, Miss Cheryl, your father assures us he's got no enemies and knows of no one who might want him dead. To be quite candid, I've considered the possibility that this might be some kind of family matter—yes, I know it's a long shot, but I'm trying to show you that we haven't been entirely idle. Major Cheryl says there are no secrets or problems about his estate—it would be shared between your mother, your sister and yourself; I imagine you would want us to rule out all three of you.'

'Yes, of course.'

'And you can't think of any conceivable reason why we shouldn't?'

'No, of course I can't.'

'And you've no other ideas?'

Jill paused. 'No,' she said. 'Have you?'

David Taylor gave her a long, appraising look. 'Personally, I think the chances are that the ads were inserted by a spiteful person who dislikes your father for some petty reason—or a reason that would seem petty to us. It could well be the man on the motor-bike. However, the probability is that the car crash and the near-accident in Oxford were coincidences.' He waited to see if she would object to his statement. When she didn't, he continued. 'The last ad's now been published. I suggest you make your father take every reasonable precaution for the next couple of weeks. There could be another incident, but I don't honestly believe anyone intends to kill him. After all, people who really intend to commit murder don't often advertise the fact publicly in advance, do they?'

Jill Cheryl shook her head. To her surprise she felt less fearful, less helpless, less certain that something dreadful was about to happen. She supposed it was part of the Inspector's job to reassure people. Nevertheless, he had been very kind, and she had taken up a lot of his time. She stood up.

'Thank you for explaining things to me. I'm sorry if—'

'Are you going back to Farlingham today or—'

They had spoken together. Now they both stopped and laughed. Jill answered his unfinished question.

'Yes. I'll have a quick lunch, then drive down.'

David Taylor hesitated for a moment. But it was a long time since he had been so attracted by a girl. She could only refuse.

'I was thinking of a drink and a sandwich in a pub myself,' he said. 'I wonder if you'd care to join me.'

David Taylor enjoyed his lunch and so, he hoped, did Jill. Stirred into action by her obvious anxiety, he called James Lindsay, who somewhat reluctantly made an appointment to see him that afternoon. 'Not that I've anything to report,' Lindsay said shortly.

Lindsay was an older man than his partner, somewhat more flamboyant in dress and less businesslike in appearance. His room was book-lined like Beckett's, but on the floor below.

'I don't mind admitting I was tired and irritable when you telephoned this morning, after that frightful flight from New York. We were stacked over Heathrow for at least fifty minutes. But I was furious, too. I hate the idea that anyone's been using my name—the firm's name— like this. We've seen everyone on the staff, and grilled them.'

'Grilled them?' said David Taylor. 'I thought the atmosphere here was probably a little more subdued than usual. What did you establish?'

'Not much, except that Lindsay & Beckett stationery seems to be scattered over the Home Counties. No one admits to having heard of Major Cheryl except those who noticed the ads, and none of them associated the campaign with Lindsay & Beckett. Just for the record, I repeat that we've got no book of that name — or anything like it — on the stocks. We've searched through the list of manuscripts we've received, and we've had nothing with a title like that in the last five or six years. The whole thing's as much a mystery to us as I suppose it is to this Major.

'Look, Chief Inspector,' he went on, 'Gladys Lee, my editorial assistant, talked to some of the girls herself, and she's had more time to think about this than I have. You met her when you were here last time, I think. She's pretty smart, though she's no beauty. We were talking a few minutes ago, and I'd like you to hear what she's got to say.'

He pushed a button on his desk, and in a moment Gladys Lee came into the room. Lindsay waved her to a chair and she sat down. Again David Taylor noticed her curiously dowdy garments.

Lindsay said, 'Gladys, you've met Chief Inspector Taylor. Tell him what you were saying to me earlier.'

Gladys Lee paused, looking from one man to the other. 'Frankly, in the first place, I don't think it's unreasonable that so many people should have some of the firm's paper. A lot of us work at home — I know I do — and it's useful to be able to write the odd letter. And once the paper's out of the office, anyone could get hold of it — friends of friends of friends; there's really no knowing where it might get to. I suspect the same thing applies to any kind of business letterhead or stationery.'

'I'm sure you're right,' said Taylor. 'I don't think there's much future in trying to track down a few sheets of your paper. And you were right about the typing,' he added. 'It certainly wasn't done on one of your office machines, if they're all like the samples you gave me, but on one of a quite different make.'

'I was certain it wasn't one of ours,' said Gladys Lee. 'And, James, as far as your signature's concerned, anyone you wrote to could have copied it, or anyone could have taken a letter or a copy of a letter — from anyone you wrote to. You see what a broad field that opens up. There's really no reason to think that anyone in the office is involved in any way.'

James Lindsay sighed, partly with relief. 'That's just where we'd got to when you arrived, Chief Inspector,' he said. 'Can you think of anything else we can do?'

'Not at the moment,' said David Taylor. 'Let's leave things at that until we see what happens. Take no more action unless you hear from me again.'

For the second time Taylor nodded to the acid receptionist, and walked out of Lindsay & Beckett's offices into the quiet Bloomsbury square. He had sounded authoritative enough, he thought, but he was still vaguely dissatisfied, and uncertain whether he was doing the right thing in treating the affair so informally. But there's no crime yet, he repeated to himself, and no real evidence there's going to be one. We can only wait and see.

This placid policy was to come to an abrupt end the next day, Tuesday, the first.

'Drat,' said Mrs Hodgeson to herself as the front doorbell rang. She was running late. She had to get home soon; Fred, her husband, would be wanting his dinner. But she must finish cleaning that bit of silver first. She hurried from the kitchen into the hall.

She opened the door to a motor-cyclist in black leathers and a yellow crash helmet. His machine was parked in the drive behind him.

'Yes? What is it?' she said.

'Parcel for Cheryl.'

'Thanks.'

She took the parcel from him and put it on the hall table, hastening back to the kitchen as Aileen Cheryl came down the stairs.

Aileen was going out to lunch. Nina Dawlish had invited her to meet some people who might be prepared to contribute their names and their money to a charity she favoured. She was looking forward to the lunch, especially as she was happy with her appearance. Her summer suit was new, very plain but extremely expensive. On these occasions it was important to create the right impression; amongst other things that meant arriving, unflurried, at just the right moment.

But the grandfather clock at the bottom of the stairs was always five minutes fast. Aileen picked up the parcel, and saw that it was addressed to 'Major and Mrs T.H.W. Cheryl'. She was mildly curious, as the parcel, quite heavy and about the size of a large book, had no return address or shop's name on the label. The name and address were typed and the parcel was very neat and sealed with self-adhesive tape. Deciding she had time to open it, she took it into the sitting-room.

She slit the tape with a nail file and removed the brown wrapping paper which, in accordance with her usual practice, she folded carefully and put in the drawer of an escritoire. She was an ardent conservationist. A cardboard box was exposed.

In a way, it was a pity it was not Jill who was at home that morning. She might have been more careful than her mother. But Aileen had never really been able to take the advertisements and the so-called 'incidents' seriously. Anyway, without thinking twice, she jerked at the tightly-fitting lid. And, of course, the bomb exploded in her face.

In the kitchen, Mrs Hodgeson heard what she later

described as 'a big shaking noise'. She dropped the silver teapot she was cleaning and dashed into the sitting-room. Aileen Cheryl, or what was left of her, lay half on the sofa, half on the floor. She was strangely blackened, and there was a horrible smell of charred flesh. Mrs Hodgeson whimpered.

She tore off her apron and threw it over the remains of Aileen, but it didn't altogether conceal the dreadful object. And the curtains had caught fire. She ran screaming from the house.

Luckily she blundered into a sensible neighbour almost immediately, and the emergency services were commendably efficient. The fire brigade and the police arrived within minutes. The small blaze was quickly extinguished. An ambulance took Mrs Hodgeson, suffering from shock, to hospital in Oxford. Dr Carson was summoned to take a first look at the body, and the forensic pathologist was soon on his way from the city. The bomb squad was notified, and a scene of crime team arrived.

Eventually, after the preliminary routine had been carried out, all that was left of Aileen Cheryl was removed to the Oxford mortuary, to await the post mortem. The Cheryls' sitting-room was sealed and the house placed under guard, while the police took stock of the situation.

The news spread rapidly through Farlingham. Some people had heard the explosion, of course. Fred Hodgeson, finding no hot dinner at home, came in search of his wife, and immediately sought consolation at 'The Birds', on his way to the hospital to find her. He was one source. Another was Nina Dawlish. Telephoning to ask why her luncheon guest had not arrived, she was told by an incautious constable that Mrs Cheryl had been killed in a fire. The doctor called the vicar, who immediately offered his services. They told their wives, and the wives told their friends. Of all the local people the only two who were not very soon aware of the event were Major Cheryl and his daughter, both thought to be in London for the day.

Aileen Cheryl hadn't been particularly popular in the village, but few people actively disliked her. Besides, such a dreadful death was shocking, especially in a small community like Farlingham. It was no act of God, but a deliberate murder—even if the wrong victim had apparently suffered. And with a bomb of some kind! What would happen next? Tom Cheryl was still alive, and those curious advertisements and the various 'accidents' must now be taken as deadly serious—literally deadly serious. What would the police do about it all?

In fact, the police authorities made up their mind with no difficulty at all. Sometimes provincial forces were reluctant to call in the Yard, but the Chief Constable of the Thames Valley force was a sensible man without false pride. As always, his resources were stretched, and this matter was clearly complex, and had ramifications that extended beyond his jurisdiction. Bombs, after all, were national concerns these days. And the ads that seemed to be related to the affair had almost certainly originated in London, or at least attempts to trace their origin would have to start there. What was more, the Metropolitan Police had already shown some interest in this Major Cheryl and his recent accident. If ever there was a case that justified his asking for help from the Yard, this was it. And the sooner the better. He reached for his phone.

CHAPTER 7

'So that's it,' said Chief Superintendent Harris. 'It's all yours, at least to start with.' It had been about half past four in the afternoon of the same day when David Taylor was called to the presence. 'For once the locals have had enough sense to call us in right away. They seem to be pretty competent, too. They've had their own scene of crime boys on the spot since this morning, and the bomb squad since this afternoon. The only thing they've had to do is move the body to Oxford. The bomb chaps want the PM results as soon as possible to help trace the type of device. But there are photographs, of course. And I can't see that it matters much. As far as I can gather, there wasn't a great deal left of her, and there's not much doubt about the cause of death.'

'There's no possible, conceivable doubt about identity, is there, sir?' said Taylor.

'No. I know what you're thinking. But no. There were only the two of them in the house. This Mrs Hodgeson and Mrs Cheryl. The Hodgeson woman almost saw Mrs Cheryl take the parcel into the sitting-room. She's in hospital in Oxford, as I think I said, but they've managed to have a preliminary chat with her. She's supposed to be shocked, and I expect she is, but she seems to have some wits about her.'

'And Major Cheryl's not been told yet?'

'No. We can't find him. That's clearly the first job, and you'll have to do something about it before you leave for Farlingham. He's said to be staying at his club, but though he looked in there for a couple of minutes this morning they've not seen him since. I imagine he'll be back later. Then there's that daughter. We've had no luck there either, though we sent a WPC Sergeant round to her address.'

'Yes, sir.' David Taylor swallowed his feelings. His first, instinctive concern had been for Jill. It was, he had to admit, not strictly professional. He forced himself to concentrate.

'I'll take Drew as usual, I think, sir.'

'Yes, sure,' said the Chief Superintendent. 'You find the Major, then get down to Farlingham. Take him with you if you like — and his daughter, if she's in London; the old boy'll need someone to look after him tonight. Now, what about this end? You'd better arrange for a team to turn over those publishers in the morning. You said that so far there's only been an internal enquiry into those wretched ads. They probably missed something, and the ads must be near the heart of the matter. We've got something to get our teeth into now, remember — a murder case — though it looks as if we've got the wrong body on our hands. Anyway, pull out all the stops. Maybe we've been a bit remiss in taking things so easily till now.'

'Yes, I agree,' said Taylor. 'And we'll have someone check the Major's service record at the Ministry of Defence. Which raises —'

'I know. I know. Terrorists. I've already had Special Branch on the blower. It's early days, or hours yet, but all I can say is no one's claimed any responsibility so far. And no group or individual has ever led up to planting a device in such a devious way, at least to my knowledge. We'll just have to wait till the bomb boys give us an opinion. But I'll be hellishly surprised if this doesn't turn out to be some kind of private enterprise.'

'Fine, sir,' said Taylor. 'I'll get started. You said the locals will meet me at the house, however late it is.'

'That's right,' said Harris. 'They're mounting a twenty-four-hour guard on the place, and there'll be a uniformed Inspector on duty with it. They're quite prepared to provide protection for Cheryl. They know we should all look damn stupid if some villain got at him now, after warning us by getting his wife in error.'

'We've had a good deal more warning than that, sir,' said David ruefully. 'What I can't quite understand is why this whole campaign should culminate in such an ambiguous effort.'

'Yes,' said Harris. 'I see what you mean. How the hell could he believe it was certain that Cheryl himself would open the parcel? Well, we'll just have to bear that angle in mind.'

'Yes, sir, of course. I'll keep in touch.'

'You do that,' said Harris. And he added, as a parting shot, 'This could be a big job for an officer of your rank, bu we're short of Superintendents and at least you've met this family. Do your best and we'll back you up as necessary. It's a chance for you, David. Make good use of it.'

'Yes, sir,' said Taylor again, closing the door of the Chief Superintendent's office.

Back in his own room, David sent for Drew and briefly outlined the situation.

'Get a car, but we'll do without a driver for the moment. We'll be staying overnight at least. Ring Kidlington and make sure there's a room for us, preferably in Farlingham. Ten minutes?'

'Yes, sir.' Brian Drew grinned. He was essentially an urban type, but a few days in the country at this time of year were just the job.

David Taylor cleared a few papers from his desk, collected his murder bag and the suitcase he always kept packed in the office and went down to the car park. Sergeant Drew was waiting.

'Everything under control?'

'Yes, sir. We're staying at a pub called the Golden Hind

in Farlingham. It's said to be pretty posh. We're to go straight to the house. A local Inspector will meet us there, and the Chief Constable will see us in Kidlington in the morning. The body's been taken to Oxford and the cleaning woman's in hospital there, too.'

'Yes, I know. Good. Now let's try the Major's club.'

As the car left Scotland Yard and glided into the evening traffic, David Taylor tried to relax. It was useless to start forming hypotheses at this stage, much better to keep an open mind. He'd been wrong, horribly wrong, when he told Jill Cheryl that her father's life was in no danger. He didn't intend to do any more guessing.

It took ten minutes to reach the club in St James's. Inside, the night porter had just come on duty, but the day man—the head porter—was still in the building. They both assured him that Major Cheryl was not there, and hadn't been there all day, except for a few minutes in the morning.

'But you're expecting him? He's spending the night here?'

'I'd have to check the book to be sure, sir.'

'Then please check. It's very important.'

'And I'm not supposed to give out information about members, sir. You could ask the secretary, but the office is shut now.' The night porter regarded him blandly. 'Who shall I say called, sir, when—if—the Major comes in?'

'Detective Chief Inspector Taylor, Metropolitan Police.' He showed them his Warrant Card, aware of the quick glance they had exchanged at the mention of the police. 'Look, have you any idea where Major Cheryl might be? There's been a serious accident at his home in Farlingham, and he's needed there urgently.'

'Well, in that case, sir,' the older, more senior porter said, 'the Major did leave a telephone number where he might be found. At least they might know where he is.'

He wrote a number on a piece of paper, and passed it across the counter of the porter's box.

'Thanks.'

Why the hell couldn't they have come out with that before, David Taylor asked himself. But I suppose that's what a club's for, he thought, to get a bit of privacy.

'Is it all right if I use one of the club's phones?'

It was a rhetorical question. He was already striding towards the row of phone-boxes at the side of the hall. At least, in a club, most of them should be in working order. He dialled the number he'd been given. Someone said hello, and he asked for Major Cheryl.

'May I have your name, please?' It was a woman's voice, low, husky, pleasant.

'Detective Chief Inspector Taylor.'

There was almost no pause before the Major came on the line. 'Cheryl speaking.'

'Sir, this is David Taylor. I'm afraid I've some bad news for you. There's been an — an accident at your house, and a small fire.' He went rushing on, hoping to forestall questions. 'What I'd like to do is pick you up — and Miss Cheryl if she's available and wants to come — and drive you down to Farlingham. I can tell you exactly what happened when I see you. Is that all right?'

'Yes, of course.' The Major was brusque. 'I assume it's serious, or you wouldn't be getting in touch with me like this. This accident — was anyone hurt? Aileen, my wife, is she — ?'

But David Taylor had interrupted. 'If you'll tell me where you are, sir, I'll be with you as quickly as possible. I don't want to waste time on the phone.'

There was a short silence at the other end of the line, then the Major said, 'Where are you now?'

'At your club, sir. They gave me your number.'

Another pause, then, 'I see. Very well. I'm at my daughter's flat.' He gave an address. 'It should take you—what—fifteen or twenty minutes to get here?'

'About that, sir.'

'Right.' The Major rang off quickly.

The Chief Inspector thanked the porters and went out to the waiting car. He got in beside his sergeant and told him where to go. It was Jill Cheryl's address all right, but the number he had telephoned was not the one that Jill herself had given him during their lunch yesterday. He wondered why Tom Cheryl had bothered to lie about his whereabouts.

'David Taylor here.'

'Would you like to come up, or shall we—'

'I'll come up, if you don't mind.'

Jill released the outer door of the block of flats, and waited in her hall until David Taylor rang her bell. Her father had arrived only minutes before. His explanation had been succinct, but far from comprehensive. She could understand that he wouldn't want David to go to Jean's house, but she didn't understand about the fire. Was it arson? Had someone—her father's unknown enemy—made an attempt to burn the house down? She had tried to ask, but her father swept her questions aside impatiently.

'For God's sake, Jill. Wait. Taylor will be here any minute, and he'll tell us exactly what's happened.'

And now he was here. She opened the door. Her mouth was dry and she felt hollow with apprehension, but she managed a calm smile. If she was surprised to see two men, she didn't show it.

'This is Sergeant Drew, Miss Cheryl. He's going to drive us down to Farlingham.'

Jill nodded. 'Come along in. Dad's in the sitting-room.' She led the way.

Tom Cheryl was helping himself to a whisky. He turned to the Chief Inspector, who introduced the Sergeant.

'Drink?' said the Major.

'No, not for me, thank you, sir. But—please do.' Brian Drew refused too.

Taylor looked from the Major to Jill. He said, 'I think we'd all better sit down for a moment, if you don't mind.' Then, when they were seated, Jill and her father on a sofa, Taylor facing them in a chair, Drew unostentatiously at the side of the room, he continued, 'I'm sorry to say we have very bad news for you. Mrs Cheryl is dead. The only consolation I can offer is that it must have been very quick.'

Tom Cheryl drew in his breath sharply. A variety of emotions flew across Jill's face, shock, disbelief, acceptance—and fear. But neither of them showed any signs of being overcome by grief. That didn't altogether surprise David Taylor. From what he knew of the two Cheryls he guessed that both of them were accustomed to keeping their feelings under control. Anyhow, he was far too experienced to believe that people reacted to crises in any established pattern.

Jill was the first to speak. 'How—how did Mother die? In the fire?'

'No. The fire was slight, incidental. A package containing an explosive device was delivered to the house and—' involuntarily he looked at the Major, but Tom Cheryl had turned away and was pouring himself another whisky—'and that's all we know for the moment,' he concluded.

'But you assume this—this device was intended for me? The death of Major Cheryl, advertised for early this month, was due today—the first. And Aileen . . .'

Abruptly Tom Cheryl buried his face in his glass and gulped whisky. It was a long time ago now, but he had once loved Aileen deeply. She had been a beautiful girl. He remembered their wedding day, and the day their first child had been born. They'd been happy then, very happy. Ironically, it was only when he'd been retired from the army, and their financial position had improved so dramatically, that things had begun to change. He drew a deep breath. Whatever had gone wrong between them, he could never have wished her dead, and that she'd died like this — in his place — was somehow obscene. It made him feel guilty, though clearly he wasn't to blame.

'That's what it looks like, sir, yes,' David Taylor said. 'Enquiries are only just starting, of course, but at first sight there doesn't seem much doubt.'

'Where is she now — my wife?'

'In Oxford, sir. We'll have to ask you to identify the body tomorrow, and there'll be an inquest in a day or two. It'll be a formality, I'm sure, and very quickly adjourned.'

Tom Cheryl straightened his shoulders. 'Right. The best thing to do now is get down to Farlingham, I imagine. I take it the house is habitable?'

'Yes, sir. I gather so.'

'Well, we're ready. Shall we go?'

They were in the downstairs hall when Jill suddenly stopped. 'I'm sorry. I must go back. I'm not sure if I turned the stove off.'

David Taylor looked at her in surprise. There had been no sign or smell of cooking in the small flat, and the kitchen door had been wide open. But there was no reason for him to object. He waited on the pavement with Sergeant Drew until Jill reappeared.

'Thanks,' she said. 'I was wrong. There was nothing on.'

'Good.'

He didn't comment on the time it had taken her to check the stove, but saw her into the car, then got in next to the sergeant. As she settled herself in the back beside the Major, he heard her say quietly, 'I phoned Jean, Dad.

I thought she should know.'

The Cheryls' private arrangements were, for the moment at least, their own, Taylor thought. But he couldn't help but be curious. First, the Major had lied to him, and now Jill had gone out of her way to deceive him, albeit in a petty way. Almost certainly it was quite innocent, but he wished she hadn't.

By the time they left London it was after eight o'clock, and it was nearly dark when they reached Farlingham. They went directly to the Cheryls' house, where a constable with a well-trained but suspicious Alsatian was in the drive. A uniformed inspector was waiting for them in the house. Tom Cheryl braced himself. The guard dogs, the boarded windows of the sitting-room that he'd seen as they came up the drive, the faint disturbing smell, left him ostensibly unmoved. He was able to pull a shutter over his feelings. Jill, though so much younger and more resilient, was less able to control herself. She was shaken by a sense of personal outrage.

'How could they?' she said. 'Damn them, whoever they are. What right has anyone got to do this to us?' There were tears in her voice, even a note of hysteria, as she went automatically towards the door of the sitting-room.

David Taylor moved quickly to intercept her. 'I'm sorry,' he said, 'but we've had to seal the room where it happened. You'll be able to go back in tomorrow or the next day.'

She looked at him blankly. 'Yes,' she said. 'I understand.'

'We've got men guarding the house, sir,' said the local inspector quickly. 'Are you going to spend the night here? Would you mind if we used the kitchen and the facilities in the house?'

'No, no, not at all. Do anything you want,' said the Major. 'We shall be all right. I doubt if we shall sleep much anyway. Jill, why don't you get us some tea or coffee and — and a sandwich, perhaps — that's all I can face.'

'All right, Dad,' replied Jill. She looked questioningly at the police officers.

'No, not for us, thank you,' said David Taylor. 'We've got quite a lot to do here before we go. And we'll make sure our hotel leaves something out for us. I suggest you go upstairs when you've had something to eat, and leave us to it. You'll be well looked after.'

'Yes,' said the Major. It was hard to know what he was thinking. 'And the morning?'

'We'll pick you up and take you to Oxford. Would nine-thirty be all right?'

'Yes. That would be fine.'

'Thank you, sir. Then goodnight to you both.'

'Goodnight.'

David Taylor glanced at Jill, but all he saw was her back as she went into the kitchen. She didn't reply.

Sergeant Drew broke the seals on the sitting-room door. Most of the lamps in the room had been smashed in the explosion, but the police photographers who had been at work earlier had been instructed to leave their lighting equipment behind. In their blinding glare the once pleasant room, stretching from the front of the house to the french windows leading on to a broad terrace at the back, appeared at first sight as a shattered ruin. The part of the room where Aileen had been standing when she opened the parcel was a shambles. Broken glass littered the blood-stained carpet, on which the routine chalked outline stood out vividly. A painting had a great slash in its canvas, and a display cabinet that had contained fine china was in pieces. In fact, a great deal of the apparent damage was due to smoke and water, but the smell of devastation lingered.

'Open the french windows and let's get some air in here,' David Taylor said. 'I take it the bomb boys have got all the bits they want,' he added enquiringly to the local inspector, who nodded. 'Well, we'll have a good look round ourselves. Just tell us the tale again, briefly to start with.'

'I guess you've heard most of it, sir,' said the uniformed man. 'It really wasn't hard to establish what must have happened, especially when they let us have a word with Mrs Hodgeson. A parcel was delivered about noon this morning by a chap on a motor-bike, not by the regular postman. He was all in black, with a yellow crash helmet. Mrs Hodgeson put the parcel on the hall table. Mrs Cheryl brought it in here, and presumably opened it. We may get more in the morning from Mrs H., though I doubt it, but at the moment she's under sedation. Incidentally, we've started a local house-to-house, without result so far, but I guess you'll want to extend the area tomorrow. We've set up a temporary incident room in the Parish Hall—that's next to the church nearby—and we're getting extra phones connected tomorrow.'

'That's all fine,' said David Taylor. 'But what about the parcel itself? Does anyone know how it was wrapped and addressed?'

'According to Mrs H., the chap just said, "Parcel for Cheryl," and handed it in to her. She didn't really look at it, because she was in a hurry, but she thinks it was wrapped in plain brown paper.'

Taylor and Drew started to look round the room. It was unlikely that the scene of crime team and the bomb squad had missed anything of importance, but they had to be sure.

'What about this?' said Sergeant Drew suddenly. He had been looking through the drawer of an escritoire which had escaped major damage, presumably through some vagary of blast. 'There's a whole drawer full of wrapping paper here. They seem to collect it. But this bit was on the top, and the rest is mostly from stores, or has stamps and return addresses.'

The paper was standard brown manila wrapping, sold by the sheet in any stationer's in the country. It bore traces of self-adhesive tape. The plain white label was typed—on a non-electric machine, probably a portable, thought Taylor—with the address: 'Major and Mrs T.H.W. Cheryl, Spring Grove, Stafford Road, Farlingham, Oxon.' If the paper had wrapped the bomb, the wording of the label cleared up one point; in the car the Major had pointed out that it would have been most unusual for his wife to open mail addressed to him alone.

'It's possible, Brian. Well done,' David Taylor said. 'But if this was the wrapping, I still don't understand why it was addressed to both of them, unless our joker really didn't care which of them he got. We'll have to check it out in the morning.' Drew put the folded sheet carefully into a plastic bag. Taylor added, 'I think that'll do for tonight. We'll have another look tomorrow.' And then, to the local inspector, 'When all the experts have finished, I'd be grateful if you'd get the worst of this mess cleared up before we let the Cheryls back in. It would be pretty awful for them to find that sickly mess beside the sofa.'

'Of course, sir.'

They sealed the sitting-room door again, had a word with the sergeant in charge of the men guarding the house and got into the car.

'Drink and food, in that order, Brian,' Taylor said. 'Let's see what the Golden Hind can provide. Will you join us?' he added to the local inspector.

'If you don't mind, no,' said the inspector. 'It's getting late. My car's here. But I'll look in at Headquarters, and if there's anything urgent I'll call you at the hotel.'

'Fine,' said Taylor. 'And thanks for your help. If we don't hear from you we'll see you at Kidlington.'

The Golden Hind lived up to its reputation. It produced an excellent meal in a small private room, and a bottle of wine on the house. But if the Chief Inspector had hoped to forget the Cheryls' troubles for an hour or two, he was out of luck. They had just finished coffee when the proprietor arrived.

He was a man in his mid-forties, well-dressed and suavely-mannered. He introduced himself as Colin Bell-Smith. David Taylor took an instant dislike to him, but tried not to show it. Bell-Smith asked if he might join the detectives, and offered them liqueurs. Sergeant Drew excused himself, saying he was tired and was going to bed, but the Chief Inspector accepted a brandy. It was a scene the two of them had played before, knowing from experience that people sometimes talk more readily when they're just one of a couple.

'Nice man, that,' Bell-Smith said as soon as the sergeant had left.

'Very nice,' David Taylor agreed, resenting the hotelier's patronizing tone. He waited.

Mr Bell-Smith seemed to have some difficulty in getting to his point, if he had one. He sipped brandy, and produced a pæan of praise for Aileen Cheryl. A splendid woman. So public-spirited. Always ready to serve a good cause. True to say she'd be sadly missed. Very, very sad she should — go — in such an — an unfortunate fashion.

'You knew her well? They came here often?' David Taylor prompted as the eulogy wound to an end.

For a moment the hotelier's face registered faint surprise, then he said, 'Mrs Cheryl, yes. She would often drop in with friends for a drink. Not infrequently she had a meal here. Mr Taylor, you must understand that a house such as this can be greatly helped by the goodwill of the more influential local families. The tourist trade is all very well, but it's not year-round. Mrs Cheryl knew a lot of people, and she was always very kind, very helpful. But the Major now, he was different. He preferred to drink with the villagers in the pub — the Duck and Drake, or "The Birds," as they call it. Not that he's been there much since those advertisements started appearing.' He gestured at the Chief Inspector's empty glass. 'Another brandy?'

'Thank you, no. It's been a long day. I think I'll turn in, if you'll forgive me. I've got an early start in the morning.'

'Yes, yes, of course. You'll need to get on with your detecting. That's really what I wanted to ask. Can we look forward to an end to all this fuss soon, now that Scotland Yard's been called in? I mean, a murder in the village, and perhaps another to come — the murderer obviously got the wrong person, don't you think? — it's all bad for business, you know.'

'Bad for business?'

'Yes. We've had one cancellation already. Mrs Dawlish was bringing a party to dine this evening, but of course she cancelled it. She and Mrs Cheryl were great friends.'

'Mrs Dawlish, yes.' David Taylor made a mental note of the name. 'That's a shame. We'll certainly do our best to clear things up as soon as possible.'

'I'm grateful. If I can be of any help —' Mr Bell-Smith left the sentence unfinished. 'Are you sure you won't have another brandy? Do.'

The man clearly wanted to talk, so why not let him? It was only gossip, David Taylor thought, but it might contain a gem, and it would serve to round out his picture of the Cheryl family and the Farlingham scene. Reluctantly he resigned himself to a drink he didn't want.

'All right. Thank you very much.'

Later, as he went to his room, he decided it had been rather a waste of effort. He had certainly learnt nothing of immediate value. But it seemed that much of Tom Cheryl's private business was known to the hotelier, including the facts that he always spent Tuesday nights in London, and visited his sister in Oxford on Fridays. If all this was known to Bell-Smith, it was probably common knowledge in Farlingham. David Taylor yawned. There was a lot to do in the morning.

CHAPTER 8

David Taylor and Brian Drew met at breakfast.

'What's the programme, sir? You don't want me to come to Oxford with you, do you?'

'No. Have a look at the Incident Room, and stay in touch with it in case I want you. Take a stroll round the village with your ears flapping a bit. Come opening time, try the other pub, the Duck and Drake. It seems to be kind of down-market, but it's the Major's favourite. See what the locals are thinking, if they'll talk. If they're anything like that man Bell-Smith, they will.'

'Fair enough, sir.'

'You'd better print that bit of wrapping paper you found, not that it'll do much good, I guess—motor-cyclists in full gear usually wear gloves. Then I'll take it to Oxford and see if Mrs Hodgeson recognizes it. I'll send it up to the Yard from Kidlington. The lab boys can probably tell if it was used to wrap explosives, and they can identify the kind of typewriter used for the label.'

'There's one thing, sir. I've been thinking—this chap's uncommonly sure of himself, isn't he? I mean, he didn't allow for any more ads. It never seems to have occurred to him that he might get the wrong person.'

'There's more to it than that,' said Taylor. 'The real trouble's that wretched label, if we have found the bomb wrapping. Our friend might have taken a calculated risk—perhaps he thought the Major would be less suspicious of a package addressed to both of them. But in that case, why deliver it on a Tuesday? It's certainly no secret locally that the Major goes to London on Tuesdays, and it wouldn't have been hard for any outsider to discover.'

'But if he did know, and still delivered it on a Tuesday addressed like that,' said Drew, 'it suggests he was really after Mrs C., and the ad business was a smokescreen.'

'Or if the motive were revenge of some kind,' added Taylor, 'he might not have cared which of them he killed. Remember, the Major could easily have come to a sticky end in that car crash—unless that really was a coincidence, or something went wrong with the plan. Anyway, it's early days yet, and we're not even sure we've got the right bit of paper. If it did wrap the bomb, it's a miracle it wasn't destroyed, and we should bear in mind that our chap would have expected it to be destroyed. It could be important for just that reason.' Taylor got up from the table. 'I'll see you at the Parish Hall in half an hour. Okay?'

'Okay, sir,' said Drew.

Fifty minutes later Jill Cheryl opened the door to David Taylor. She looked tired, as if she hadn't slept well, but not as if she'd been crying. Taylor looked at her doubtfully, suddenly distrusting his own emotions.

'Are you all right, Jill?'

'Fine, thanks—David.'

It was the way she said 'David' that put him in his place, he thought a little bitterly. They were on first name terms, and had been since they'd lunched together an æon ago, though for some obscure reason he'd addressed her as 'Miss Cheryl' when she opened the door of her flat to him last night; maybe it was the formality of the occasion, or the presence of his sergeant, he thought. But now, in some curious sense, they seemed no longer friends; they had become opponents—on opposite sides? Why should that be? Damn it, he'd got nothing against her father.

'Shall we go right away?' she asked.

'Sure,' he said. He stopped short. 'Are you coming too?'

'Yes, if you don't object. I want to see Mrs Hodgeson, and I don't feel like driving.'

He smiled at her. 'Of course I don't mind. Come along.'

In Oxford they went first to the mortuary, where Major Cheryl identified the body of his wife. Jill was persuaded to wait in the car. The Major had seen death often enough, and in various guises, but it was a harrowing moment for him. He didn't exactly faint, but suddenly everything became unreal, and he found himself sitting in a chair in a passage with David Taylor offering him a glass of water.

'I wish this were something stronger, sir. It's a nasty experience.'

'I suppose you've got used to it. I thought I had.'

'I don't think one ever does, sir.'

A certain icy tone in the Chief Inspector's voice made Tom Cheryl give him a swift glance. The good-looking face was set, the mouth a thin, bitter line, the jaw jutting as if to receive a blow.

'I always see my wife and daughter,' David Taylor said softly. 'They were killed by a drunk driver while they were waiting at a bus stop.'

'I'm sorry. I didn't know. Jill didn't tell—'

'I don't usually mention it.' He hadn't told Jill. The occasion hadn't arisen, and it wasn't something he spoke of readily, but he was glad she would know now. 'If you're feeling up to it, sir, we might push on to the hospital. Then I'll drop you both at your sister's house on my way out to see the Chief Constable at Kidlington.'

'Yes, of course. Thank you. Poor Mrs Hodgeson.'

In fact, Mrs Hodgeson was having the time of her life. Never before had so much attention been showered on her. Fred had made the effort to come and see her. And the doctors, nurses, police, everyone had been terribly kind. She even had her own private policewoman sitting beside her bed. And now here were the Major and dear Miss Jill, with a nice young man. At the sight of Jill she began to remember, and her face started to crumple, but Jill bent over and kissed her on the cheek.

'Mrs Hodgeson, we're enormously glad you weren't hurt. You're not to worry about anything. We'll come and collect you as soon as you're well enough to go home, and we'll make sure everything's all right—'

'Oh, Major Cheryl! How could anyone be so wicked?'

Hurriedly, to prevent the incipient tears, Jill introduced the Chief Inspector. Mrs Hodgeson was distracted, and duly impressed. So, when the Cheryls had left, was David Taylor. Mrs Hodgeson was a voluble witness, but an observant one. The man who had delivered the parcel had just said, 'Parcel for Cheryl'—she was positive of that. He was about the Chief Inspector's own height, young, and thin—kind of lanky. It wasn't Mrs Hodgeson's fault the description was so inadequate. The black leathers and the yellow helmet had provided an excellent disguise. She was sure he hadn't taken his gloves off. And she produced one other bit of information.

'I seen him before,' she said. 'Leastways I think I have. I couldn't swear to it, not with him being in that garb. But the day the Major's old boxer died I seen him riding along the road not far from the house. If it wasn't him, it was someone very like him.'

David Taylor showed her the piece of brown wrapping paper. As he expected, she was uncertain. 'It certainly could have been,' she said, 'but I didn't really look at it—the parcel or the label, I mean. All I wanted was to finish the silver and get along home.'

Taylor spread out the paper and refolded it in what seemed the original creases, in order to demonstrate the size of packet it might have wrapped. 'That looks about right,' she said, 'but I couldn't swear to it.'

The Chief Inspector thanked her profusely. But, as he returned to the car where Tom Cheryl and Jill had waited while he interviewed Mrs Hodgeson, he had to admit she hadn't really helped much. He had an unhappy feeling of frustration about this case.

His frustration was not dissipated by his visit to the Kidlington Headquarters of the Thames Valley police. The Chief Constable was welcoming and cooperative as far as facilities were concerned; he was even prepared to allocate some of his precious men to keep the Major under surveillance while he was at home or near Farlingham. But he was singularly unhelpful with ideas. He'd called in the Yard, and that was it. It was up to the Yard to do what was necessary, and then get off his patch.

'If you don't mind my putting it bluntly,' he said, 'you don't call for a dog and then bark yourself. In any case, it's pretty clear the key to this thing's in London. There's nothing in Major Cheryl's local life to provoke an attack like this, is there?'

'Not as far as I know,' said Taylor.

'Well, my secretary next door has assembled all the reports we've had so far — copies have gone to the Incident Room at Farlingham, of course — but we thought you might like to have a look at them here first, in case of any queries. Get him to give you a room and put you in touch with anyone you want.'

'Very well, sir,' said Taylor, accepting his dismissal. 'I'll report daily, and see you again by the end of the week, if not before.'

He found the secretary, and was quickly installed in a spare office, with a telephone and the file before him.

He went to work at once. A phone call to London established that a team was still at work at Lindsay &

Beckett's. It was confirmed that none of the typewriters in their offices—all similar electric models—matched the electric machine on which the letter to the newspaper and the sheets of advertising copy had been prepared. None of the staff admitted to owning electric machines, though many had portables or manual office models. There were no other useful results. Did the Chief Inspector want searches of the homes of all the staff, or should they leave that for the present?

Taylor thought for a moment. Maybe most of Lindsay & Beckett's staff would cooperate, but a few might demand search warrants. It really wasn't worth the effort at this stage. What was more, it might alert someone unnecessarily. 'No,' he said. 'Leave it. I'll let you know. But keep all the typing samples you've taken. I've got a typed label I want you to check, though I'm sure it was done on a manual machine.'

The initial report of the bomb squad was in the file. It served merely to demonstrate that anyone with an 'O' Level knowledge of chemistry could make a simple yet powerful device. In fact, the bomb seemed to have been too simple in design and construction to suggest any terrorist connection, and its method of delivery—by hand rather than through the mail—was most unusual by current terrorist standards. The bomb experts were inclined to agree with the Chief Superintendent at the Yard that this one represented private enterprise. And this view was reinforced by the details of the Major's service career, which revealed no grounds for thinking that any group might still be seeking him, so many years after retirement.

Asked about the wrapping paper, the experts claimed that it might well be possible to say if it had been used to contain explosives. Told the size of the package—obtained from the creases in the paper—they agreed that it sounded about right for the extent of the explosion.

Taylor promised to send the paper for laboratory examination.

And that was all. It could hardly be less satisfactory. Taylor phoned Farlingham and learnt from Drew that so far no one else had seen a motor-cyclist at any of the relevant times. Neither had a re-examination of the shell of the Mini yielded any further evidence. He sighed and put down the receiver. Slowly he got up from the desk, and went in search of his car and the Major and Jill.

CHAPTER 9

If Chief Inspector Taylor felt frustrated by the lack of results from the police enquiries in the days following Aileen Cheryl's death, it was nothing to the frustration suffered by the Major. There was a twenty-four-hour guard on his house. This irked him, though he was prepared to accept it for Jill's sake. But he couldn't go into the village or for a walk through the lanes without being conscious of discreet eyes watching him. He had absolutely refused to have any kind of overt personal bodyguard, but Chief Inspector Taylor was equally adamant that he must accept some surveillance, at least until after the funeral.

'It's a bloody waste of effort,' the Major said angrily. 'If this chap intends to kill me too, he will. You won't stop him.'

'Nevertheless, you must let me try, sir.' David Taylor was patient. He knew that what the Major said was perfectly true but, quite apart from professional pride, he was determined to do all he could to prevent another death. He was growing to like Tom Cheryl — and his daughter even more. 'If only we had some clues as to who might have a motive . . .'

And the questions began again, though there was nothing the Major could add. At last he said, 'Look, we've been over this time and time again. As far as I can see there's no reason on earth why anyone should want me dead, and go through all this ridiculous and spiteful business to achieve it.'

'Sir—' said David Taylor.

'Let me finish,' said the Major. 'You know my background—it's an open book: public school, Sandhurst, regular army. I refuse to believe I've got any enemies left from World War Two; I've never served in intelligence or the kinds of jobs where you make obscure enemies, and my service was over long before terrorism became popular—at least the kind of terrorism that leads to this sort of thing. And you can write off my career since I left the army. I suppose you could say I've had competitors, and they call the City a cut-throat place, but company directors don't very often go round actually cutting each other's throats. If they did, I hope they'd be a bit more effective than this chap.'

David Taylor was pleased that the Major could manage to look at the situation a little less seriously. He was going to make encouraging noises when Tom Cheryl continued, 'Naturally, I'll go on thinking about it, but I doubt if I'll come up with anything more helpful.'

'Thank you, sir,' said David Taylor. He didn't have much hope either, but he had to appear grateful. He knew the Major was trying to cooperate, but it was clear that this line of enquiry, like all the others, had come to a dead end.

'Well, if that's all for the moment, I ought to be answering some of those letters of condolence. But first I think I'll go for a stroll in the garden. It's a glorious morning.' Tom Cheryl stood up. 'You'll find Jill in the kitchen if you'd like a cup of coffee.'

Leaving David Taylor, he went out through the

conservatory. He needed to think, to make up his mind about his future. It wasn't like him to vacillate. But somehow he couldn't really believe that Aileen was dead. He still expected to see her walk into the room, or hear her commanding voice on the phone. It wasn't that he missed her particularly — a fact that made him feel a little guilty sometimes — but her presence seemed still to permeate the house.

He had read somewhere that life after bereavement didn't become real again until the funeral was over, and perhaps things would be better after tomorrow. But he didn't want to think about it; in a way, he was dreading it. The inquest had been simple — a true formality, its ritual shielding its meaning, over very quickly — a certificate issued and the enquiry adjourned till further notice. Tomorrow would be quite different. First there would be the church service — he had told Edwin Galverstone to lay on whatever he thought best — and after that the committal. Dust to dust. Ashes to ashes. With everyone standing around and gawking, from the Carver twins and their village cronies to Nina Dawlish, and Jill and himself. Not to mention the police, and probably the press. Then back to the house for — what? Jill had insisted that the traditional baked meats were essential.

Thank God Celia wouldn't be there. Jill wasn't exactly tough, but there was steel in her. His other daughter wasn't made of the same stuff — and now, about to produce his first grandchild, couldn't be expected to attend.

But he mustn't rely too much on Jill. It wasn't fair on the girl. Anyway, the new term would be starting soon and she'd have to go back to London. She couldn't be allowed to abandon her job and her career for his sake. He could always get a housekeeper or, if Mrs Hodgeson would come in more often, he might manage for himself—if he decided to stay in Farlingham at all. There was nothing to keep him here except a few casual friends, and the garden. He didn't even have to consider Sal anymore. He could take a flat in London, be near Jean. He smiled as he thought of Jean Aubyn.

Aileen Cheryl died on a Tuesday, and was buried on the Tuesday exactly a week later. The day was fair and fine, belying the nature of the occasion, as Tom Cheryl watched his wife's body being lowered into the ground in the churchyard at Farlingham. The Major's eyes were downcast, his mouth set. He was willing the Reverend Edwin Galverstone to hurry up and get it over.

He had thought the funeral would be an ordeal, but he had not really expected it to be so much of a public show. He was horrified by the size of the crowd that had filled the old church and overflowed into the churchyard. The family was there, of course, though they were very much in a minority. Neither he nor Aileen came from prolific stock. There were a few personal friends and associates, mainly from London. The villagers had turned out in force, including Mrs Hodgeson and others he knew well. There were the police; the Chief Constable had come, with David Taylor and Brian Drew. And there was a representative selection of media men, though by this time the name of Cheryl had largely disappeared from the front pages and the TV bulletins.

All these people, if not entirely welcome, were at least explicable. What Tom Cheryl couldn't understand was the number of individuals and groups, smartly dressed and, to judge from their cars, well-to-do, who were unknown to him. They seemed to be acquainted with each other, and to know Nina Dawlish, whom he accepted as a friend of Aileen's, and that man Bell-Smith from the Golden Hind. He found it difficult to believe that all these people were connected with Aileen's committees and good works, but he supposed that must be so.

Lost in thought, Tom Cheryl felt the pressure of Jill's hand on his arm, and he lifted his head. The vicar was coming to the end of the committal service. The Major smiled at his daughter.

And at that moment came the unmistakable crack of a shot.

A woman screamed. A photographer had the presence of mind to take a shot of Tom Cheryl's face, eyes wide, mouth half open, a startled man. Police seemed to be everywhere. The Reverend Galverstone, who had faltered for only a moment, continued the final prayers.

'Amen,' he said in an unnaturally loud voice.

There were few responses. After the sudden silence that had followed the shot a breath of murmurs had spread like a wind, ever increasing in volume, amongst those gathered in the churchyard. The resulting babble offended Edwin Galverstone's sense of decency. He hurried to the side of his friend. But Chief Inspector Taylor was ahead of him.

Fingers digging into the Major's elbow, the other arm hard round Jill's shoulders, David Taylor said, 'Home, sir, please. Quickly. Both of you. Your family and friends will follow. We'll cope with the rest.'

However politely phrased, it was a clear order, and Tom Cheryl did his best to obey, if only because of Jill. But he was delayed by those wishing to offer a word of sympathy, to shake hands. He couldn't ignore—he refused to ignore—the landlord of 'The Birds' or Fred Hodgeson, proud of the part his wife had played in the recent tragedy, or the local vet, or others like them. And in the event it didn't matter.

By the time the police had established that the sound of the shot had come from an automatic bird-scarer in a neighbouring field, normally turned off on such occasions, but unfortunately forgotten on this one, the Cheryls' drive was blocked with cars. Mrs Hodgeson, who had slipped away immediately after the service in church, had already let some people into the house, and more were arriving. Most of these were unknown to Tom Cheryl, for the more tactful of his friends had paused to allow him to get home first.

'Who on earth are all this lot?' he said to Jill in the hall. 'I thought we agreed to ask only the family and close friends back to the house.'

'We did, Dad. I suppose they're Mother's friends and just assumed they should—'

She was interrupted by Tom Cheryl's sister, who had come from Oxford with her husband. 'Tom, what's the matter? Why are you waiting out here? You must come and greet these people. I don't know them.'

'Yes. Yes. All right.'

The Major led the way from the hall. He had scarcely been in the sitting-room since Aileen's death. Quite apart from the damage after the explosion, some vague feeling of what was seemly had made him prefer to use his study. All the arrangements had been left to Jill, and he drew a sharp breath as he entered and saw the room's condition. The glass had been replaced in the windows, but there were no curtains. The walls and part of the ceiling were either smoke-stained or newly-plastered; there had not yet been time to complete the redecoration. Some of the furniture had disappeared, and a picture he had liked. The place looked bare, strange, alien.

'It was the best we could do in the time, Dad,' Jill said hurriedly, seeing his expression. 'We had to use it; none of the other rooms is big enough.'

'It's fine.'

More people were coming in behind them. The room, though far from small, was beginning to look full. The two girls, nieces of Mrs Hodgeson, who had agreed to help out, were having difficulty passing amongst the guests with their trays of canapés and glasses of sherry. There was a babble of conversation, laughter. It was as if everyone had forgotten the reason for being there.

For a moment or two Tom Cheryl, almost unconsciously, found himself part of this near-cocktail party. He began to circulate, like any host. Then suddenly it became obvious to him why at least some of these people had chosen to encroach on his hospitality. He saw one man draw a line with his finger on a patch of smoke-blackened wall, to the amusement of the young girl with him; for a second the line looked to Tom like the first stroke of a capital 'A'. Another couple were pointing to the damaged escritoire. Then Colin Bell-Smith deliberately lifted a corner of the rug that covered the bloodstains on the carpet.

It was the last straw—the funeral, the shock of the sudden seeming shot, these people, and now this. The Major strode across to the hotelier. 'Mr Bell-Smith, as far as I know you were not invited to my house. If you've satisfied your curiosity I should be glad if you'd go.'

'Well, really! I've never been so insulted—'

There was an immediate silence in the room, but Tom Cheryl was too angry to care. He turned to the man who had marked the wall. 'That goes for you, too, whoever you are.'

A girl giggled. Nina Dawlish took it upon herself to intervene. 'Adrian's a friend of mine,' she said.

'But not of mine,' Tom Cheryl retorted. He looked round the room and saw Jill, with David Taylor beside her, watching him anxiously. He got a grip on his temper. 'I'm sorry. But this was meant to be a small gathering of relatives and very close friends. Those of you who were invited to my house are very welcome, but I should be grateful if those of you who came—out of misguided curiosity, perhaps—without being asked, would leave.

I'm sure you won't want to intrude.'

It was, in the circumstances, a pleasant enough speech, but there was a murmur of protests, denials. Colin Bell-Smith was the first to go, ostentatiously circling Tom Cheryl. Others followed quickly, embarrassed. Some muttered apologies. Nina Dawlish hesitated, then stormed out, proclaiming loudly that though she'd been asked she had no wish to stay, and would never enter the house again.

'And that's something to be thankful for, I suppose,' said Edwin Galverstone uncharitably. He had come across the room to stand beside his friend.

'I suppose so,' said Tom Cheryl wearily. 'I'm sorry,' he said again. 'I shouldn't have done that. It was everything together — it was all too much for me. But it was foolish. I shouldn't have done it. I certainly don't need to make more enemies.'

CHAPTER 10

After the funeral, interest in the Cheryl affair seemed to wane. The Major left for London to stay with his daughter, who was due back at her school. The police appealed for any information concerning a yellow-helmeted motor-cyclist seen in the Farlingham area on the Tuesday the bomb went off, or during the preceding month. There were, of course, a lot of yellow crash-helmets in the neighbourhood, and their owners were all laboriously questioned and exonerated. The Chief Inspector and his sergeant disappeared from view, and were known to have given up their rooms at the Golden Hind.

In fact, as David Taylor frankly admitted at a series of conferences in Kidlington and at the Yard, the police were at a loss. Apart from the reported motor-cyclist, the only concrete piece of evidence that had come their way was the bit of brown wrapping paper that Sergeant Drew had found in the escritoire. The laboratory admitted to indications that it might have been used to wrap the device. On this assumption, the arguments concerning the label and its address were reviewed again in detail, but little could be added to the views expressed by David Taylor and his sergeant at breakfast the morning after the explosion.

It was confirmed that the label had been typed on a portable manual machine—almost certainly an oldish Remington—and a debate was in progress among the authorities as to whether they should show their hand by taking samples from all typewriters owned by anyone associated with the case, including the whole of Lindsay & Beckett's staff. As far as Lindsay & Beckett were concerned, the decision was to wait a while. Gladys Lee had pointed out, with truth, that there was no evidence, apart from a readily available piece of letterhead, and the apparent forgery of Lindsay's signature, to tie Lindsay & Beckett to the crime at all. Nor was there any reason to suspect anyone at Farlingham, though enquiries would be made there to determine who owned portable typewriters and their makes.

In the light of all this, the possibility of double-bluff was naturally considered. Could Aileen Cheryl have really been the intended victim, and the advertisements merely designed to mislead? If so, the Major himself would be a prime suspect, of course, but no one had any ideas about a credible motive.

For reasons he himself only half understood, David Taylor made no mention of the Major's lie concerning his whereabouts on the day of the explosion. He had traced the phone number he had been given at the Major's club to a Mrs Jean Aubyn—presumably the 'Jean' whom Jill had phoned from her flat before leaving for Farlingham that evening. Mrs Aubyn was a well-known book illustrator, and thus could be said to have some connection with the publishing trade. But there seemed nothing untoward in the connection between the Major and Mrs Aubyn—it was, after all, clearly well known to Jill—and David Taylor felt reluctant to probe unless he was forced to.

It was the rumour and its aftermath that finally made him take action. No one was ever clear where the rumour started. Probably it had more than one source. But start it did, immediately after the funeral, though it failed to reach the attention of the police for some days. It spread rapidly, growing in malice, as rumours do. It reached Farlingham vicarage via the sexton, who heard it from the Carver twins, and who passed it on in a somewhat expurgated form to Mrs Galverstone. She, in turn, having made a few tactful enquiries amongst her friends and acquaintances, told her husband.

'Edwin, have you heard this extraordinary story going around about Tom Cheryl?'

'No. What is it now?' After the Major's cutting remarks about encouraging gossip, the Reverend Galverstone was a little sensitive on the subject. Besides, he was busy writing a sermon; he made it a point of honour to create his own rather than depend on one of the many services available to clergymen.

'They're saying he's glad Aileen's dead, that he didn't get on with her and—'

'Who are "they"?'

His wife shrugged. 'People in the village and—and others. The story seems fairly widespread. Even a visitor staying at the Golden Hind, who hurt his ankle and had to go and see Dick Carson, mentioned it.'

'Doctors shouldn't discuss their patients.'

'Oh, Edwin, for heaven's sake!' Dorothy Galverstone could be exasperated by her husband's determined charity. 'Dick Carson wasn't discussing a patient. It was she who—'

'They'll be saying Tom murdered Aileen next—'

'They're saying that already.'

'What?' Edwin Galverstone thrust his papers away, took off his reading glasses and stared at his wife. 'Dorothy, are you serious?'

'Perfectly serious. If it's not being said in so many words, at least it's being implied.'

'But how? Why?'

'Various reasons. Either he wanted her money. Or she wouldn't give him a divorce. Or he was just plain tired of her. Take your choice.'

'Absolutely absurd—all of them! Dear God, how long has this been going on? Why haven't I heard about it before?'

'Probably because you're known to be a friend of Tom's.'

'And now's the time to prove it! This damnable rumour's got to be quashed—and preferably before Tom gets back from London. He's been through enough recently without having his character assassinated as well.'

It is easier, however, to start a rumour than to stop one, though when Tom Cheryl returned to Farlingham on the Monday after the funeral it was not at first apparent to him that a subtle change had taken place in the villagers' attitudes to him. He was relaxed and comparatively cheerful, after a week spent largely with Jean Aubyn. The horror of Aileen's death had receded. But he wasn't inclined to be sociable. Once or twice he had supper with the Galverstones, but he didn't go to church. Instead, he went for long walks, thankful to be no longer under police surveillance, but he didn't drop in at 'The Birds' on his way home. He missed Sal, more than he cared to admit. He didn't miss Aileen.

Mrs Hodgeson took extra care of him, so that the household, simple as it was, seemed to run itself. He didn't realize the significance of her attention until, coming in from the garden one morning, he heard her on the telephone.

'Shut up! Shut up! You're a wicked bugger!'

It was too late for Tom Cheryl to withdraw, to pretend he hadn't heard. Mrs Hodgeson had seen him. Banging down the receiver, she turned to face him. There were spots of colour high on her cheekbones. It was not the sort of language she was accustomed to use, and she was ashamed to have been overheard by the Major.

'Trouble, Mrs H.?'

'You could say that, Major Cheryl, sir. Yes.'

'Would you like to tell me about it?'

Mrs Hodgeson dried her hands furiously on her apron, but inspiration didn't come. There was no way of telling her employer, kind as the Major was, that someone kept telephoning to say filthy things about him, to say he'd killed his wife, and they should bring back hanging for him. She drew herself up to her full height of five feet two.

'I—I would prefer not, sir.'

'All right, if it's a personal matter.' Tom Cheryl hesitated. He was no fool, and he was prepared to make a guess at what had caused such an outburst from Mrs Hodgeson. 'But if it concerns me, you should tell me,' he said gently. 'Was it someone threatening me again?'

'No. It wasn't threats.' Mrs Hodgeson avoided meeting his gaze. 'Just—just dirty things. Wicked lies. Several times it's happened.'

Suddenly Tom Cheryl felt cold. His guess had been wrong. Not threats. Dirty, wicked lies. Somehow they

seemed worse. But he couldn't bring himself to question Mrs Hodgeson further. He managed to smile.

He said, 'Don't worry, Mrs H. It must be some crank. If he doesn't stop, I'll go to the police or get the number changed. Meanwhile, don't answer the phone. Or, if you must, and it's this chap again, put down the receiver at once. Don't try to argue with him. Then he'll get tired of it very quickly.'

'Whatever you say, Major.' Bobbing her head, Mrs Hodgeson retreated towards the kitchen. She was at the door when she turned and added, 'My Fred says there are rumours going round the village, too.'

Hurriedly she shut the door behind her, and stood with her back against it, her heart thumping against her ribs. Well, she'd told him. It was up to him now. He knew what was going on, and perhaps there was something he could do about it. It wasn't fair. He was a good man, a kind man. People shouldn't tell such wicked lies.

Mrs Hodgeson's remarks had left Tom Cheryl disturbed, but not fully comprehending. The letter that arrived the next day made clear what she had only hinted. It was typed, and had been posted in Oxford. It read, 'Major Cheryl, you are a murderer. You killed your wife Aileen. You made her die a horrible death. You deserve to die but, as God is merciful, we'll be merciful too. If you leave the country quickly, we will not inform the police.' Needless to say, the letter was unsigned.

Telephone calls. Rumours in the village. Now this revolting accusation. As if what had gone before hadn't been bad enough. Angrily Tom Cheryl tore the letter into small pieces, and dropped them in the wastepaper basket. Whoever had written it must be sick. Best forget the whole thing.

But it wasn't easy to forget. If Jill had been at home he might have discussed it with her, but the school term had

begun and she was back at work. Anyway, she would have wanted to tell David. Catching himself thinking of Chief Inspector Taylor by his first name, he smiled wryly. He must have picked up the habit from Jill, who seemed to be seeing a lot of the young man. Tom Cheryl sighed.

He wanted Jill to be happy, more than anything, and he'd been enough of a nuisance recently. He wasn't going to worry her with this dirty business. The same applied to Jean. This was a bad time for all of them and—

The shrilling of the telephone interrupted his thoughts, and he hurried to answer it. 'Hello, Cheryl here,' he said automatically.

'Murderer!' a voice said, a man's voice, but obviously disguised. Then the receiver was banged down.

Tom Cheryl rubbed his ear, and swore. The phone rang again. He eyed it malevolently. He would like to ignore it, but that wasn't possible with Mrs Hodgeson in the house. Holding the receiver well away from him he cautiously gave his number.

'Major Cheryl?' It was a different voice.

'Yes.'

'Major Cheryl, my name's Hooper. I'm an estate agent in Oxford. I deal in properties such as yours and as I gather you're thinking of selling, I took the liberty of—'

'How did you gather I'm thinking of selling?'

'Well—' Mr Hooper hesitated, then his confidence returned. 'I was so informed, sir. I'm sorry if I've jumped the gun, as it were, before you were ready I mean, but I've a prospective buyer for you. If the house is what he hopes, he's prepared to make what I consider a very good offer in the circumstances.'

'In what circumstances?'

Hooper could have kicked himself, but he had to reply. 'People don't fancy buying a house where there's been a murder,' he said bluntly. 'If I were you, Major Cheryl, I'd jump at a good opportunity to get rid of it.'

Tom Cheryl curbed the retort that sprang to his lips. He said quietly, 'Thank you for your advice, Mr Hooper. If or when I think of selling my house I'll let you know.'

He hung up, cutting off Mr Hooper in mid-sentence. He was less polite to the second and third agents who phoned later in the day. And in the evening, when he dropped in on the Galverstones unexpectedly, he said with brutal abruptness, 'What's this rumour that's going around about me?'

Edwin Galverstone, startled, exchanged glances with his wife. 'What—what rumour, Tom?'

'That I'm selling the house and leaving Farlingham.'

'Oh, that.'

'But you're not—'

They spoke in unison, obviously relieved he'd not said what they feared he might. He looked from one of them to the other. Suddenly he laughed aloud.

'Oh dear,' he said. 'You know, I didn't kill Aileen.'

'We never for a second believed you did,' Dorothy Galverstone said indignantly. 'But—but it's what some people have been saying—and how does one stop them?'

He told them about the telephone calls and the anonymous letter. It was good to have it all out in the open, to be able to discuss the matter, to have other opinions, even if the situation remained unaltered.

'What do you think? Do you think it's the same joker?' he asked.

The vicar shook his head. 'No. In my view the man who put those advertisements in that paper intended to kill you, Tom. He killed Aileen in error, and that's frightened him off.'

'Or perhaps he thinks he's punished you enough,' Dorothy Galverstone intervened.

'Punished me? What for?' Tom Cheryl was surprised. 'The man must be mad.'

'Sometimes people brood on minor or imaginary ills till

they do go round the bend,' Mrs Galverstone said.

'But they don't suddenly descend to anonymous letters and phone calls,' Edwin Galverstone added. 'No, Tom. This is small-time malice, the work of a petty troublemaker. It doesn't have the stamp of the same man.'

Tom Cheryl sighed resignedly. 'You're probably right. The problem is what to do about it. I hate the idea of going to the police again, and it's absurd to have an unlisted phone number in a place like Farlingham. Besides, that wouldn't stop letters. Wait and see is the answer, I suppose. With luck he'll get tired of it, and these hideous rumours will die down of their own accord.'

Luck, however, was not on Major Cheryl's side.

Another letter had been written. It reached the Yard the following Friday. Harris summoned David Taylor.

'Any more progress with the Cheryl affair?' the Chief Superintendent asked abruptly.

'None since our last conference, sir, and my last report. There's been no further attack on Major Cheryl or his property, and none of our leads have come to anything. We're doing our best, but at the moment the case seems pretty dormant, I'm afraid.'

'Not quite.' The Chief Superintendent reached into his in-tray and took out an envelope. 'You'd better read this.'

David Taylor looked at the envelope. Grey-coloured. Thick, expensive stationery. First class mail. Posted in Farlingham. Addressed to the Chief Constable in Kidlington, who had clearly forwarded it to the Yard. He extracted the letter and ran a thumb over the address at the top of the paper. It was heavily engraved. The handwriting was large and florid. This was no scruffy tip-off. He read carefully, his face impassive.

The Grange,
Near Farlingham,
Oxfordshire.

Dear Sir,

I feel compelled to write to you on the subject of Aileen Cheryl's murder. Mrs Cheryl was a remarkable woman in the time and devotion she gave to charitable causes, and she was also a close personal friend of mine. I must say at once that I am appalled by the casualness, if not the downright negligence, that the police have shown in the investigation of her death. For example, no one has ever asked to interview me though, I repeat, I was a close personal friend of the victim, and might have provided valuable evidence.

At present, from what I gather, the police have lost all interest in this case. Presumably they are content to allow Mrs Cheryl's death to become yet another unsolved mystery. I am not so content. This is why I am writing to bring to your attention the following points.

There is a body of opinion among Mrs Cheryl's friends and acquaintances which holds that the parcel bomb may always have been intended for her, and not for her husband. Certainly the murderer appears satisfied with the present situation. The alleged attacks on Major Cheryl have ceased.

As to who might have wished Aileen Cheryl dead, I would not willingly point a finger at anyone, but I feel it my duty to ask you to arrange for a senior police officer to call on me as soon as possible. At the very least I can then tell him of some of the circumstances of Mrs Cheryl's private life that I believe to be relevant to her death. I should add that others will substantiate what I shall have to say.

The letter was signed, 'Yours faithfully, Nina Dawlish.'

The bitch, thought David Taylor, the nasty, interfering old bitch. All she wanted to do was cause trouble for the Major, and she looked likely to succeed. Aloud, he said, 'I suppose what she really means is that she's going to accuse Major Cheryl of plotting to kill his wife. You know we've thought of that, sir, but there's no evidence, no motive, at least not an obvious one.'

'She maintains we haven't looked for any evidence, and to some extent she's right. I know we've discussed it briefly, but we haven't dug, have we?'

'No, sir,' David Taylor agreed miserably. The wretched Dawlish woman was going to cause trouble for him personally, as well as for the Major. Jill wouldn't take kindly to the idea that the police were seriously investigating her father. 'It was always a hell of an outside chance.'

'And one you don't believe in,' said the Chief Superintendent. 'Nor do I. Nevertheless, we'll have to dig a bit now. This bloody woman's a taxpayer, and it looks to me as if she's out for her pound of flesh, preferably the Major's. It was her friends that caused the Major's outburst after the funeral, wasn't it? Maybe this is their way of getting back at him. But you'd better go down to Farlingham tomorrow and hear what she and her chums have got to say. Then we'll take it from there.'

'Damn! Tomorrow's Saturday, sir. Can't it wait?'

'No. Not a chance. Sorry if it mucks up your weekend, but the Messenger case comes up at the Old Bailey on Monday and—'

The Chief Superintendent went on to talk of other matters, and David Taylor was thankful when at last he was able to get back to his own office. He telephoned Jill immediately, but there was no answer, and he swore under his breath. He realized that a lot more was at stake than his plans for the weekend.

Between them, Harris and Nina Dawlish had certainly mucked up these plans—a drive with Jill to Richmond for lunch, a quiet supper in a Chelsea restaurant when he planned to ask her to marry him, then home, with all he hoped that might imply.

But could he conscientiously investigate suspicions that Major Cheryl had murdered his wife, if he himself were committed to the Major's daughter? Because he was committed to Jill. He looked at the pale band of flesh on the third finger of his left hand. He had loved Elizabeth very much, but he couldn't grieve forever.

It was the traditional policeman's dilemma, though it hadn't yet come to a choice between his career and Jill. Not yet. He tried the phone again, and this time she answered. 'Jill, I'm most terribly sorry, but I can't make tomorrow. I have to go down to Farlingham. The Chief's orders.'

'Farlingham? Why?' Her voice was sharp with anxiety. 'David, nothing's happened to Dad, has it?'

'No. He's fine,' David hastened to reassure her. 'It's just something that's come up.'

'What sort of something? A lead?'

'Possibly.' There was silence at the other end of the line and he went on, 'Jill, I can't go into it on the phone.'

'No. I understand.' Which meant she damn well didn't. 'How long will you be down there?'

'I don't know. I'll call you just as soon as I know, and as soon as I get back.'

'Yes, of course. David, I must go. There's someone at the door. Goodbye.'

She rang off and he found himself staring wretchedly at a dead phone. Damn. Damn. Damn. She had known at once that something was wrong, sensed his restraint and withdrawn from him. But there was nothing he could do about it now—except apply himself to clearing up this business of Nina Dawlish as quickly as possible.

It was well after six on a Friday night, but Chief Inspector Taylor sat down at his desk, reached for the file labelled 'Cheryl' and started to reread it from the beginning. Unfortunately, it gave him nothing to cheer about.

CHAPTER 11

The Grange was an imposing house, long and low, built of beautiful cream-coloured Cotswold stone. Its driveways were well-kept, its lawns closely manicured, its flowerbeds immaculate. A gardener was spraying the rose-bushes and to one side, in stables where a couple of hunters occupied loose-boxes, a chauffeur could be seen polishing a Rolls. Clearly there was no shortage of money here—or of staff.

And the opulence extended to the interior of the house. A butler opened the front door to Chief Inspector Taylor and Sergeant Drew, and showed them into what he called the morning-room. It was almost the size of David Taylor's flat, and definitely larger than the ground floor of the sergeant's surburban semi-detached. The furnishings were modern, as were the paintings, but none of it had come cheap. David Taylor, who knew a little about pictures, recognized a Hockney and a Riley, and there was a very fine Hepworth bust.

'And old man Dawlish describes himself as a "company director"?' Sergeant Drew, who was never overly impressed, said. 'What do you suppose that means?'

David Taylor had made a few enquiries. 'Retired property magnate. Got out at the top of the boom. Filthy rich.'

'Why the close friendship with Aileen Cheryl? It's a bit odd. The Cheryls aren't in this class.'

'Nowhere near, I'd say.' David Taylor nearly added, 'Thank God.' 'I guess the two women met through some charity do. Mrs Dawlish might have been a patron, and perhaps Mrs Cheryl was useful to her. Maybe they liked each other, too.'

David Taylor looked at his watch. They had arrived on the dot for an appointment with Mrs Dawlish, but evidently she didn't intend to offer them the same courtesy. In fact, it was twenty minutes before she arrived. Nor did she apologize. She gave them one glance and, as soon as introductions had been completed, said, 'There'll be no need for you to stay while we talk, Sergeant. Manson—' she nodded towards the butler who had reappeared—'will show you to the kitchen and Cook will find you some coffee, or some beer if you prefer.'

The Chief Inspector's head snapped up and his mouth opened. But the sergeant frustrated his protest, winking hugely at his superior. He said, 'Thank you, ma'am. That would be very nice.' He didn't quite touch his forelock, but the gesture was implied, and David Taylor's spurt of anger was drowned by his desire to laugh.

'Now you sit down, Chief Inspector, and we can discuss the reason for your visit—the sad death of Aileen Cheryl,' Mrs Dawlish said firmly, pointing to a chair.

David Taylor sat, as ordered, and listened while Mrs Dawlish elaborated on what she had said in her letter. He was glad of the opportunity to study her and assess her value as a witness. She was not quite what he had expected.

In appearance she was not unlike The Grange itself. A black-haired petite woman, she was well-preserved, carefully groomed, obviously expensive. But she was nobody's fool. She had a quick turn of wit and a practical approach. In spite of her autocratic behaviour David Taylor found himself, if not liking her, at least giving her a grudging admiration. When she said she had been fond of Aileen Cheryl, he believed her. When she added that she bore the Major no ill will, he also believed her. She showed no sign of being either mean or vindictive, but she was obviously a stubborn woman determined to get her own way, and she had made up her mind that Aileen Cheryl's death should be avenged.

'I have no wish to accuse anyone,' she said, 'but I must speak frankly, Chief Inspector. The Cheryls' marriage hadn't been happy for some time, and recently it had sadly deteriorated. Aileen herself told me that she was actually becoming afraid of her husband.'

'Really? Did she say why?'

'Well, they drifted apart as so many couples do, but they didn't separate. At first because of the children. Then, by the time the girls had grown up and left home, they had seemingly got used to the status quo. Aileen was no longer young, and she had her friends and her charity work to keep her busy. Tom had his garden and his dog and cronies of his own in Farlingham. And, of course, there were his London interests.'

Something in Nina Dawlish's voice alerted the Chief Inspector. She was about to confound him, or she thought she was. He gave her his full attention.

'London interests? You mean in the City? Directorships, that sort of thing?'

'Yes. And his mistress.'

David Taylor was not altogether surprised, but he put a query into his voice, 'His mistress?'

'Oh, come, Chief Inspector, the thought must have occurred to you. You're a man of the world, surely. You must know the old indulge themselves as well as the young.' Suddenly, she became serious. 'But I'm afraid, in this case, it might have been a motive for murder. You see, though Aileen no longer loved Tom as she once did, she wanted to keep him as her husband. She wouldn't give him a divorce. I don't think she believed in it, for one thing. She was a religious woman. She went to church regularly. But in addition she had her pride. It's no joy to be a deserted wife when you're in your fifties, and she was determined that Tom shouldn't put her in that position.'

'How could she stop him in the long run, Mrs Dawlish? The law—'

'She had him watched on some of his Tuesday visits to London, when he was meant to be staying at his club. She got all the evidence she needed.'

'For what? You said the last thing she wanted was a divorce.' David Taylor was puzzled.

'Her object was to prevent him trying to get one, and she succeeded. She didn't give me any details, but I gathered she was now able to threaten his woman with such an appalling scandal that Tom daren't contemplate a divorce or even a separation. Mind you, I have to admit she didn't stipulate that the affair must end.'

'Are you sure, Mrs Dawlish? That sounds a bit like a form of blackmail. And it's hard to imagine the nature of any such scandal. These days, after all, almost anything's soon forgotten. A move to another part of the country, or even abroad—unless she was implying something criminal.'

'I know, I know, Chief Inspector. The same point occurred to me, naturally, but I didn't like to press the matter. All I'm telling you is my understanding of Aileen's position.'

'I see,' said David Taylor. 'Do you know any names, Mrs Dawlish, or anything about this lady?'

'Aileen referred to her as Jean. That's all I know.'

Again, Taylor was not entirely surprised. He nodded glumly. If Mrs Dawlish was speaking the truth as she understood it, and there was no reason to suppose she wasn't, she had certainly provided the Major with a motive for getting rid of his wife. But motive by itself was not enough; it certainly didn't prove he had done so.

'You mentioned that Mrs Cheryl said she was afraid of her husband,' Taylor said. 'Do you know what she meant by that? Was it a figure of speech, or do you think she was serious?'

'I think she was serious,' Nina Dawlish replied without hesitation. 'Aileen told me that he'd been behaving very oddly, and she was frightened of what he might do next. For example, she caught him outside in his dressing-gown the night before he had that car accident on the road to the station, and he was furious with her. Later I think she suspected he might have tampered with the car himself.'

'Did she say so?'

'No, she didn't. But she did say his dressing-gown was filthy, and she couldn't imagine what he'd been doing.'

'Yes, I see.'

'Oh, I know most of this is hearsay, Chief Inspector, but I myself saw him on the verge of hitting Aileen the morning his dog died, as did most of the congregation at the parish church. You can ask the vicar if you doubt me. For that matter, you were there yourself when he turned Mr Bell-Smith out of his house. Poor Colin. He was dreadfully upset about that, and I'm not surprised.'

'I don't doubt you, Mrs Dawlish,' David Taylor said truthfully, 'but people interpret things in different ways, and sometimes they draw inaccurate conclusions.' He smiled to take the edge off his words.

'Does that mean you're going to do damn all about everything I've told you?'

'No. On the contrary. I assure you, Mrs Dawlish, we shall look into it all with the greatest of care. Obviously it's necessary.' And how the hell I wish it weren't, he thought.

Once clear of The Grange, Sergeant Drew parked the car on the grass verge at the side of the road, and made his report. He had been lucky. Cook had turned out to be a local woman, whose husband's sister was Mrs Hodgeson, and there was little she didn't know about the Cheryl household. From her the sergeant had learnt of the telephone calls accusing the Major of murder, the anonymous letters that Mrs Hodgeson had found in bits in the wastepaper basket, and the importunate estate agents and their offers for the house.

'No doubt someone's got it in for the Major,' Sergeant Drew concluded.

Yes, and I could make a good guess as to who, thought David Taylor. Aloud, he said, 'He's got his supporters, too, evidently, at any rate amongst the Hodgesons and their relations.' Having heard the sergeant's report he was feeling far more cheerful. He now had a good excuse for questioning the Major again, without appearing accusatory. He would prefer to do so alone.

He said, 'You go ahead to the pub, Brian, and make sure there'll be a good lunch for us, even if I'm late. Meanwhile I'll tackle the Major. You can wish me luck.'

But he needed more than luck, David Taylor realized, as the door was opened to him by Tom Cheryl. He had underrated the Major. Though he looked tired, with dark grey circles painted under his eyes, and his normally healthy skin had an unhealthy yellowish tinge, there was no doubt about his spirit.

'Come in, Chief Inspector.' He led the way to his study. 'I was expecting you.'

'You were, sir?'

Tom Cheryl smiled, without humour. 'It was pretty obvious you couldn't ignore the current crop of Farlingham rumours indefinitely. It will make it simpler if I say at once that I didn't cause Aileen's death, and I haven't the faintest idea who did. But I realize you've got to assure yourself of those facts.' He gestured to a chair. 'I was having a glass of sherry when you came. Will you join me, or is that against regulations?'

David Taylor didn't hesitate. 'Thank you, sir. I should like that.' He sat down and, to regain the initiative, said,

'I'm sorry you've been bothered by these phone calls and anonymous letters and things.'

'So am I.' The Major's voice was cold. 'If I ever catch the swine, I'll—'

'No! No, sir. Don't take the law into your own hands. That'll only make things worse. Leave it to us.'

'I know. I'll try.' Tom Cheryl took an envelope out of his pocket and passed it to the Chief Inspector. 'The phone calls seem to have ceased, but I got another of these this morning. It's the second. Posted in Oxford and much the same text. You are a murderer. Get out of Farlingham. We don't want you here. The stupid part is that I'd intended to sell the house and go—but I'm damned if I'll be driven out.'

Taylor examined the envelope and its contents with interest. Unidentifiable paper, but another typing sample. A glance showed it had probably been done on a manual machine, but one quite different from the Remington that had produced the parcel bomb label. He replaced the letter in its envelope, and put them carefully in his wallet. 'The phone calls, these letters, the estate agent hoaxes,' he said. 'It's petty persecution, not the work of the man who sent the bomb.'

'No. Edwin Galverstone would agree with you; and I think I do too. But it makes life unpleasant, and the rumours . . .'

If ever there was a right moment David Taylor sensed it was now. He hated himself for doing it, but he said, 'Sir, there's a personal question I have to ask you. Did you at any time ask Mrs Cheryl for a divorce, and if so did she refuse you?'

'That's two questions, Chief Inspector, and the answer to both of them is no, emphatically no. Where on earth did you get hold of such tales?'

David Taylor didn't answer. Either Major Cheryl was telling the truth or he was a very good actor. His surprise had every appearance of being genuine, and his answer bore the ring of truth.

'I don't pretend Aileen and I had an ideal marriage, but I had no reason to want a divorce. Why should I?' said the Major.

David Taylor drew a deep breath. 'To marry Jean Aubyn, perhaps, sir,' he said softly.

The silence in the room was suddenly acute. The tick of the clock on the mantel grew louder and outside in the garden a thrush's song was unexpectedly piercing. Tom Cheryl pushed back his chair and stood up. His expression was grim.

He said harshly, 'Chief Inspector Taylor, you have no right, no right whatsoever, to drag Mrs Aubyn into this matter. She and I have been friends for many years, but at no time has either of us considered divorcing our respective spouses or marrying each other. If you're searching for a motive for me to have murdered Aileen, you'll have to look elsewhere.'

Again, the words rang true, but so had what Mrs Dawlish had claimed. 'Mrs Cheryl was aware of this relationship of yours?' David Taylor persisted.

The Major hesitated. 'I assume she guessed there was someone, but I doubt if she cared.' It was clearly a prevarication, and Tom Cheryl clearly knew it. He passed his hand over his face. 'Christ, the law being what it is today, if I'd been determined on a divorce, Aileen couldn't have stopped me. You know that.'

David Taylor didn't volunteer the answer that Mrs Dawlish had suggested. He asked a few more questions, then took his leave and, deep in thought, walked through the village to the Golden Hind.

'Before we go any further,' he said to Drew as they finished their lunch, 'there's one bit of business we can clear up.'

This bit of business was made easier by the arrival of

Mr Bell-Smith at their table. He was, he said, delighted to see them again. Though the hotel was officially full, he would of course find beds for them for the night. He always kept one or two rooms free in case special guests turned up unexpectedly.

To Sergeant Drew's surprise, David Taylor's thanks were profuse. 'That's very good of you, very good. You've been most helpful to us. I wonder — could I ask another favour? Could I borrow a typewriter for half an hour?'

'Of course. We've a brand new Adler in the office. I'll tell my secretary.'

'Oh no. I wouldn't want you to bother her. Besides, I'm not the world's best typist. Bad for the machine. Don't you have an old portable somewhere? That would be more my mark.'

'There's the one I use myself, an Imperial portable. It's not new, but it's in good condition. I'll bring it down to the little sitting-room you used before. And I'll see you're not disturbed.'

'Thanks. And I'd also like your hotel registers going back to the beginning of the year.'

'There's only one. I always start a new book on January 1st. But why do you —'

'As soon as you can, Mr Bell-Smith, please.'

A sudden hardness in the Chief Inspector's voice stopped the hotelier from arguing. He hurried to fetch the typewriter and the register, and to check on the sitting-room. Whatever his faults, he was efficient. Within minutes everything was ready for the two police officers.

'If there's anything else you want, just ask the switchboard to put you through to me.' Bell-Smith gestured at the telephone on a side table. 'I'll be upstairs in my suite.'

'We'll call you,' David Taylor said, and held the door open for him. 'Now, Brian, while I do a spot of typing I want you to go through the register. I've been thinking, and there's something we've overlooked. If the person who killed Aileen Cheryl wasn't a local, he must have acquired a good deal of local knowledge, and one obvious ploy would be to come and spend a holiday in Farlingham, possibly here at this pub. So I want the name and address of any lone male who's stayed here for more than one night since January. I know it's a very long shot — possibly that's why it didn't occur to us before — but I'm prepared to try anything now.'

'You don't believe it's the Major, then?'

'Between you and me, Brian, no, though I'm trying to keep an open mind.'

The sergeant grinned and settled to his task. David Taylor put some paper in the typewriter — an Imperial portable, as Bell-Smith had said. For a moment he stared at the blank sheet, his thoughts on Jill Cheryl. Then he began to type, not fast but quite competently. First, he typed: 'Major and Mrs T.H.W. Cheryl, Spring Grove, Stafford Road, Farlingham, Oxon.' Then he took the Major's anonymous letter from his wallet and typed one of its sentences: 'Get out of Farlingham before it's too late.'

He also had with him a photocopy of the parcel bomb label, and he spread the three samples — the label, the letter and his own work — on the table in front of him. As he expected, two of them were identical. It wouldn't necessarily stand up in court, but it satisfied him. Before he put the documents back in his pocket, he called Drew and explained the situation.

Murderers came in all shapes and sizes, but the cold, calculating variety were made of sterner stuff than Colin Bell-Smith. Bell-Smith, as he had suspected, was the type who went in for anonymous letters and, presumably, anonymous phone calls and spiteful practical jokes. At least he could get that nonsense out of the way. He told the girl at the switchboard that he wanted to see Mr Bell-

Smith immediately.

The hotelier arrived with surprising speed. 'Yes, Chief Inspector, what can I do for you?'

'You can begin by telling me what evidence you have that Major Cheryl killed his wife, Aileen Cheryl, on the first of the month,' the Chief Inspector said formally.

Bell-Smith's mouth dropped open. 'I—I—'

'You do believe this to be true, don't you?'

Bell-Smith took a deep breath. 'As a matter of fact, I do, yes,' he said.

'Well, why? What evidence have you that has not been reported to the police?'

Bell-Smith hesitated, then: 'Why not? He could have put those ads in the paper himself, then lied about those accidents, or faked them. You've not found any witnesses to any of them, have you?' He had overcome his initial shock and now was eager to justify his accusation. 'As for the bomb, he was in the Royal Engineers when he was a soldier, so he'd have known how to set about making it. And he didn't care a damn about his wife. Everyone knew that. He neglected her horribly. He was always off to London—I suspect he had a fancy woman there—leaving poor Mrs Cheryl alone. He didn't want to mix with her friends. God knows why he thinks himself so superior to us all.'

Colin Bell-Smith's spiel came to an end. He was breathing heavily and there was a fleck of spittle at the corner of his mouth. His eyes bulged slightly. Momentarily he was overwhelmed by his own venom.

The Chief Inspector regarded him coldly, not bothering to hide his contempt. Sergeant Drew ostentatiously turned over a page in his notebook. They let the silence lengthen. Bell-Smith, still standing, began to fidget from one foot to the other.

'Is that all you have to say, Mr Bell-Smith?' David Taylor separated each word carefully. 'Are you seriously telling us that because of what is no more than sup-position you have taken it upon yourself to behave so appallingly?'

'I—I don't know what you're talking about.'

'I'm talking about wasting the time of the police in a murder case, about interfering with the police in the execution of their duty. That's a criminal offence. You could go to prison.'

'But I've done nothing.'

'You call it nothing—this hounding of Major Cheryl with threatening letters and obscene phone calls?' David Taylor mimed amazement. 'How are we to know you're not the man we're looking for? If you hate the Major so much, perhaps it was you who inserted those adver-tisements and sent him a bomb that killed Mrs Cheryl by mistake.'

'No! No! I swear.' Bell-Smith was scared. He swallowed hard. 'The letters, yes. Two of them and—and some phone calls, but nothing else.'

'The estate agents?'

'Yes, yes. I forgot them.' He was beginning to sweat. 'Yes, that was me. But not the bomb. I'd have no idea how to make a bomb. Anyway, I'd never kill anyone. I swear before God—'

To David Taylor's embarrassment a dark patch of moisture appeared in the front of the hotelier's trousers. Bell-Smith, whey-faced and trembling, had lost control of himself. The Chief Inspector looked away.

'I believe you,' he said, 'but—'

'What'll happen to me?'

'I'll have to speak to my superiors, but if you cooperate with us now they may decide not to charge you.'

'Anything. Anything. It would ruin me, ruin my business.'

'Okay.' David Taylor turned to the sergeant. 'You've got a note of all that? Good. How were you getting on with the register?'

'Almost finished, sir. I've only netted seven so far. It doesn't seem a popular place for lone males.'

'Right. Mr Bell-Smith, do you have a telephone that doesn't go through the switchboard?'

'Yes, upstairs in my suite. If you want to use it—'

'We'll be there in ten minutes,' said Taylor as the hotelier sidled past him.

'Whew!' said Sergeant Drew as the door closed. 'You were sailing a bit close to the wind there sometimes, weren't you, sir? Not that he's likely to raise a stink about it.'

'Not after he's changed his trousers,' said David Taylor, laughing. 'At least that's cleared up. Now we can start on those hopefuls you found. Seven's not a bad number. Maybe Bell-Smith can help us whittle them down. The rest will have to be checked out.'

'Right away? Before Monday? That won't be easy.'

'Why not? I'm working over the weekend. Why shouldn't the other buggers? There was some sense in what Mrs Dawlish said. We may have been taking this affair too casually.'

Sergeant Drew sighed. He said nothing. It wouldn't have been very kind to David Taylor to suggest that other men had wives and kids they liked to see sometimes.

CHAPTER 12

The next morning David Taylor went to church. It wasn't his usual Sunday practice, but before leaving Farlingham he wanted a word with the Reverend Edwin Galverstone. If, as Mrs Dawlish had said, Aileen Cheryl had been a religious woman, she might have talked to the vicar about

the possibility of a divorce. He had called at the vicarage
the previous evening, but Edwin Galverstone had been
out. After Matins seemed an excellent opportunity to
catch him. Besides, David Taylor reflected as he made his
way through the churchyard past Aileen Cheryl's grave, it
was nearly three weeks since her death — and nearly four
since he had first met Jill and her father; the investigation
couldn't be said to be proceeding very rapidly. Maybe
prayer would help.

He arrived late, expecting the service to have already
started, but the vicar was even later. Taylor slid into a
back pew, aware of the interest he was causing. The
congregation was fidgeting and whispering. Among them
he spotted Mrs Dawlish with an elderly, florid man,
presumably her husband, Dr Carson and his wife, Mrs
Hodgeson with her Fred, a few other locals he could
identify and some visitors he had seen at the Golden
Hind. There was no sign of Major Cheryl or Colin Bell-
Smith.

The organist was improvising vigorously, and David
Taylor's thoughts strayed. The list that Sergeant Drew
had compiled from the hotel register had already been
reduced to three possibles. Bell-Smith had vouched for
two as regular visitors, each over seventy years of age. Of
the other two, it had been established that one had gone
to a job in Dubai in the Spring, and the other had been
staying at the hotel with his fiancée, though they had
modestly occupied separate rooms. None of them were
starters. Probably the rest would be ruled out too. It had
always been an outside chance.

Belatedly David Taylor stood, as the music swelled and
the congregation shuffled to its feet. The vicar, flanked
by his choir boys, was making his way to the altar. The
whispering and covert glances caused by the Chief
Inspector's presence ceased. The service began.

David Taylor joined in the singing. He had a pleasant

tenor voice, and was glad to use it. He was in the middle of the last verse of the opening hymn when he felt a tug at his sleeve. He turned abruptly. A small, wizened man whom he remembered from Aileen Cheryl's funeral as something to do with the church was standing at his elbow.

'Message from the Reverend. He says it's urgent.'

'Thanks.'

David Taylor accepted the many-folded piece of paper that was thrust towards his hand. Casually he glanced around. No one seemed to be taking any interest in him. He unfolded the paper and, placing it on the open pages of his hymn book, read the message.

It was brief. 'Essential I should talk to you. Please come to vicarage after Matins. Edwin Galverstone.'

David Taylor slipped the paper carefully into his pocket. Useless to speculate why Galverstone was so eager to see him, but nevertheless impossible not to do so. He gave a mental shrug. Almost certainly it was something unimportant concerned with the current gossip in Farlingham. Still, the meeting with the vicar would serve his own purpose.

The service continued uneventfully, though the vicar had, probably intentionally, chosen a particularly appropriate text for his short sermon: 'Thou shalt not bear false witness against thy neighbour.' David Taylor wondered what effect it would have on the congregation; probably it would only serve to give the rumours a certain amount of seeming official backing.

He left the church just before the end of the service and strolled the fifty yards to the vicarage. He rang the bell, half expecting no answer, but a woman in a blue and white striped apron, her hands covered with flour, opened the door.

'Good morning, Mrs Galverstone. I'm awfully sorry to disturb you.' He smiled at her. 'But your husband asked me to meet him here after Matins.'

'Hello, Chief Inspector. I heard you were back in Farlingham.' Dorothy Galverstone wiped her hands on her apron. 'I can't think what Edwin wants. He never mentioned anything to me. You'd better come in here.'

She led him down the hall and into a room that was obviously used as an office and study. There were a lot of books, a desk and a few worn but comfortable-looking chairs.

'Sit down. He won't be long. I'm afraid you'll have to excuse me. I must get on with my cooking.'

David Taylor turned to thank her, but the words never came. Reflected in a wall mirror was a corner of the interior of the kitchen, its door half open, and for a split second he caught sight of the figure of a man sitting at a table, shelling peas. It was Major Cheryl. Taylor grinned to himself. Whatever Galverstone had to say to him, it was unlikely to be to the Major's detriment, and that at least was a pleasant change.

While he waited, David's thoughts drifted from the Major to his daughter. He wondered what Jill was doing at this moment. Coming out of church? Walking in the Park? More likely correcting exercise books and preparing for the following week. If it hadn't been for that interfering Dawlish woman, they might by now have been in bed together.

His frustrating thoughts were interrupted by the arrival of the vicar, slightly out of breath. He brought with him two small boys.

Edwin Galverstone didn't waste any time. He said, 'Chief Inspector, this is Ginger Carver and this is Ted Hodgeson, a nephew of the Mrs Hodgeson who works for Major Cheryl. They've something to tell you about the Sunday when the Major's boxer Sal was killed.'

'We seen the man what did it,' Ginger Carver burst out, unable to contain himself any longer. 'We seen him, didn't we, Ted?'

The younger, smaller boy nodded his head without speaking. He was more afraid of his mum than Ginger was of his, and he hadn't wanted to go to the vicar. But Ginger, always the leader, had insisted. Ginger had said it mattered. Even if they got a beating for playing hookey from the choir they had to tell. If they didn't Major Cheryl would be hung. The London fuzz had come back to the village to arrest him. They mustn't let that happen.

'You mean you saw what happened?' David Taylor said.

'No, we didn't. We didn't see him hit Sal and drive the Major into the ditch, but we seen him after, a guy on a motor-bike, with a yellow helmet.'

David Taylor hid his disappointment. This wasn't much help. But the boys were obviously in earnest. He had to take them seriously. He said, 'First, are you sure about the day?'

They both nodded vigorously. ' 'Twas Sunday. Vicar knows. We ought've been in Church, in choir, see,' Ginger said, 'but we went playing in the fields instead.'

'Which is why they didn't come forward before,' Edwin Galverstone explained. 'But I've promised to have a word with their mothers, and I'm sure they won't get punished this time.'

Ted Hodgeson wasn't so sure. He wished Ginger would hurry up and finish the story. If he could get to his dad and tell him all about it before Mum heard, it might be a whole lot better. 'Go on, Ginge,' he urged. 'About the guy getting into the van.'

'The van?' Immediately Taylor's interest had quickened. 'You said he was on a motor-bike.'

'He was, but he drove the bike into a van. It was like this . . .'

Ginger Carver was growing in confidence and he explained clearly how he and Ted had seen a light grey van parked inside a field and wondered what it was doing there on a fine Sunday morning. Curious, they had decided to get up close and inspect it, but a guy on a motor-bike had suddenly appeared along the lane. While they watched from behind a hedge he had ridden into the field, opened the back of the van, taken out a sort of wooden ramp and pushed the bike up it into the van. Then he had got in himself and driven away.

David Taylor beamed on the two boys. 'That's absolutely splendid information,' he said. 'Now what else can you tell me? Can you describe the chap?'

But this was beyond them. The description Ginger gave, with Ted's assistance, was as inadequate as the one Mrs Hodgeson had provided of the motor-cyclist who had delivered the parcel bomb. Nevertheless, David Taylor felt in his bones that they were one and the same man.

'What about the van?' he prompted.

That was easier. The van was light grey. There was no name painted on the side they had seen. They didn't know about the make, but it was like Ginger's uncle's van, and that was a Ford.

'Thank you both very much,' David Taylor said. He took out his wallet and extracted two one-pound notes. To his surprise the boys were shaking their heads.

'We did it for the Major,' Ginger said. 'Now you know he was telling the truth you won't arrest him, will you?'

'No,' said David Taylor solemnly, 'Indeed I won't now.'

'Super!' A grin split Ginger's freckled face. He turned to Ted, who was pulling at his sleeve. 'Lay off!'

'The number,' Ted muttered. 'The van's number.'

David Taylor had sharp ears, but he could scarcely believe them. 'You—you didn't get the number of the van?' he said.

'Yes. Ted collects them,' Ginger said nonchalantly. 'Sorry. I forgot. We wrote it down for you.' He fished in his pockets and found a dirty scrap of paper.

'Thanks,' David Taylor said. 'That's terrific.'

And it was terrific, he thought, as he walked back to the Golden Hind. It was almost the first lucky break they'd had, and it could prove a real lead. He hastened his stride. He was hungry. There had been a delicious smell from the Galverstones' kitchen when the vicar showed him out. Then his stride broke. He remembered he had completely forgotten to ask Galverstone if Aileen Cheryl—or the Major, for that matter—had ever discussed divorce. He was doubtful if it mattered. It was more important to get that van traced. He quickened his stride again.

As they agreed over lunch, Sergeant Drew's morning had been successful, too. He had news of the remaining three men on his list. One had turned out to be a fellow detective-sergeant from the Yard, casually known to him, who had won a little money on the Pools, and had decided to spend it on a posh holiday. Another was the headmaster of a boy's private school.

Neither of these visitors could be absolved entirely, but the most interesting by far was the seventh—a Philip North, who had stayed at the Golden Hind for two weeks in April. He had given a London address. The block of flats existed close to Victoria Station, but quick work by the Yard had shown that, by some quirk of architecture, there was not, and had never been, a Flat 18. On the surface, it looked like a false address, but it could have been a mistake of some kind. The local police were questioning everyone in the building. Most of the inhabitants had lived there for several years, and so far none of them had admitted to knowing, or knowing of, a Philip North. The agents for the block of flats had been contacted, and a representative was at that moment on his way to their offices, so that the records could be checked.

'I got a description from Bell-Smith,' Drew reported. 'The chap was about your height, moderate build, clean-shaven, grey-haired, aged perhaps forty. Not terribly helpful, I'm afraid. Bell-Smith was willing enough, but this was a first-time guest, and not very memorable.'

'And that was all? Bell-Smith never got into conversation with him and asked him what he did for a living?' said Taylor. 'I find that hard to believe.'

'Company director.' The sergeant grinned, his mouth full. He was enjoying his lunch, but he preferred his wife's cooking, quite apart from her company, on a Sunday. 'Which covers a multitude, as they say. Anyway, North wasn't in the district on business. He was recuperating after an operation, at least that's what he claimed. He spent most of his time taking gentle walks around the district.' The sergeant paused for effect. 'Very interested in the history of Farlingham, he was, according to Bell-Smith.'

'And in Farlingham's gossip?' David Taylor got the point at once. 'He could be, he could just be our man, though he doesn't sound much like a wild motor-cyclist. And God knows anything about motive.'

'Yes, that's one of the odd things about this case,' said the sergeant. 'No one seems to gain from the murder — unless, of course, it's the Major.'

'Which reminds me,' David Taylor said smoothly. 'they're tracing the van's number, but there's something I forgot for the moment. As soon as we get back to town we'll pay a call on Mrs Jean Aubyn and see what she has to say.'

But here, to Sergeant Drew's delight, they were thwarted. Not unexpectedly on a Sunday evening, Mrs Aubyn was out. There was no answer to her bell. When they had identified themselves, an obliging neighbour volunteered the information that she had gone away to the country for the weekend. She would be back on

Monday or Tuesday. She had left her key, as usual, but not her phone number. It was, after all, only a couple of days.

With that they had to be content.

CHAPTER 13

Thanks to the registration number so surprisingly recorded by Ginger and his friend Ted, the police had no difficulty in tracing the grey van to a used car dealer in Reading, and on Monday morning a report was waiting for Chief Inspector Taylor at the Yard. He read it, at first with only mild interest, then with amazement.

He called for Drew. 'Listen to this,' he said. 'According to the Licence Bureau in Swansea, the owner of the van is a second-hand dealer. The local police say he's not too reputable, and he claims to have sold it for cash three months ago.'

'He could be telling the truth,' the sergeant said. 'The computers at that Bureau take forever to process the paperwork.'

'He's telling the truth this time all right.' David Taylor grinned. 'No doubt about it. He sold the van to a Trevor Roberts, who gives the same non-existent address as Philip North, that chap on your list of visitors to the Golden Hind.'

Sergeant Drew whistled. 'Do we have a description?'

'Yes, sort of. But very vague, and what there is of it doesn't exactly fit with North, as Bell-Smith remembered him. Maybe we've got a gang of some kind on our hands, but let's assume for the moment that North and Roberts are the same man.'

'Seems reasonable,' said Drew. 'Do we try to pull him in?'

'No, we won't pull him in, not yet, even if we can find him. And I doubt if we can, if this is all we've got to go on. We can try tracing the van, but if he really is the chap we want he'll probably have disposed of it by now. Resold it, or abandoned it somewhere, I guess. Or he's painted it red and given it new licence plates, in which case we won't have a prayer. But we'll go through the routine.'

'Right. I'll put out the call.' Sergeant Drew hesitated. He liked David Taylor, who rarely pulled rank, and enjoyed working with him. But this case was different. He wasn't sure why. Perhaps it was because the Chief Inspector was getting involved with the Major's daughter. Certainly he seemed to be turning a blind eye to some things. 'It—it did occur to me that this guy—North, Roberts, whatever he calls himself—he's no pauper, is he, sir? He stays at the Golden Hind. We don't know about the motor-bike, but he buys a van for cash. And he seems to move round the country. It all costs money these days.'

'What are you suggesting, Brian?'

'I'm not sure, to be honest, but the Major's said to be pretty well off. If he wanted to get rid of his wife, he might have paid someone to—to organize it—and keep suspicion away from himself.' Seeing the expression on the Chief Inspector's face, the sergeant stopped abruptly.

'You mean he hired himself a kind of rural hit man or decoy, or something?' David Taylor laughed. 'Since half of Farlingham does suspect him, his plan hasn't worked, has it?' He spoke lightly, but he knew that, as long as the Major had a possible motive, the sergeant's proposition was one he should at least keep in mind. To change the subject, he said, 'The first thing is to talk to Mrs Aubyn, as soon as she gets home, and preferably before the Major's spoken to her, though I doubt if we'll manage that.'

In fact, Tom Cheryl had made no attempt to contact

Jean. He knew where and how she was spending the weekend, and he wouldn't have considered intruding unless it was absolutely essential. Anyway, there was no real need to warn her. Much as he wanted to protect her from prying questions, he had realized that sooner or later their relationship must come to the attention of the police. She had accepted that fact, too, and had said she didn't care, providing publicity could be avoided. But she knew that, all things considered, this was a pretty big proviso, and she dreaded the consequences if her name was publicly linked with the Major's, or her photograph splashed across the newspapers. Even if her husband didn't see it himself, someone would be sure to tell him.

So, although she had been half-expecting such a visit, it was with considerable doubt that late in the afternoon Jean Aubyn opened her front door to Chief Inspector Taylor and Sergeant Drew. It had been a searing weekend and, on reaching home a short while ago, she had tried to restore her flagging spirits with a quick whisky. The result had been to make her feel slightly giddy; she was in no mood to welcome the detectives with any enthusiasm.

'You'd better come in,' she said wearily, and led the way up the steep stairs to the living-room.

Following closely behind her, David Taylor admired her slim hips and shapely legs. She was a most attractive woman, he thought, though not at her best at the moment. As she turned to face them, motioning them to chairs, he noticed the downward drag of her wide, generous mouth, and the black smudges under her eyes. She was clearly under a strain.

We're sorry to intrude on you, Mrs Aubyn,' he said, 'but we're hoping you might be able to help us. It's about the death of Mrs Aileen Cheryl.'

'Well, I didn't think you'd come about the van,' Jean Aubyn said tartly.

If she had wanted to put them off balance, she couldn't have chosen a better opening gambit. Sergeant Drew caught his breath and began to cough. Chief Inspector Taylor bit his tongue in surprise.

'What van is this, Mrs Aubyn?' he asked, his voice carefully neutral.

'I'm sorry. It was just a van that parked in the mews a few times. Quite illegally, I may say. It annoyed me, and I phoned the police.' Jean Aubyn gave an apologetic smile. 'But that's not why you want to talk to me.'

'What sort of van was it?'

Jean Aubyn stared at the Chief Inspector. 'How should I know? Just an ordinary delivery van, except that it sat outside without delivering anything, and no one's meant to park there and obstruct —'

'What colour was it?'

'Grey. Plain grey. There was no name on it, but I took the number. I gave it to the police.'

'Fine! We'll get it from them.' David Taylor grinned at her. 'I suppose you wouldn't remember which days you saw this van?'

Jean looked at him in exasperation. 'Chief Inspector, what is all this about? What's it got to do with Aileen Cheryl? I only mentioned the van because — because — I was being sarcastic, I suppose.'

'I'm very glad you did, Mrs Aubyn. I'm sure your local station would have got around to informing us, but there's always a chance the information might have got overlooked.'

'What information? I still don't understand.'

'We're trying to trace a grey van, Mrs Aubyn,' David Taylor said gently. 'We've evidence which leads us to believe that the motor-cyclist with the yellow helmet — Major Cheryl has told you of him?' Jean nodded. 'That this man also possessed a grey van, which he might have been using in connection with —'

Jean Aubyn was quick, too quick for the Chief Inspector. 'You mean it was the same man? Outside in the mews? What was he doing? Watching me?'

'It's possible,' David Taylor said cautiously.'

'But that's dreadful. Why? Why should he?'

Suddenly, without warning, Jean Aubyn began to shake. 'S—sorry,' she said, but she couldn't control herself. Her teeth were chattering. She buried her face in her hands.

Beautiful, strong hands. David Taylor noticed, as he leapt to his feet and made for a table where there was a display of bottles. No brandy, but he poured her a stiff whisky, and held it while she gulped it down. She smiled wanly.

'Thanks. I'm so sorry. I've had a hell of a weekend and now—all this.'

'That's okay, Mrs Aubyn. Take your time. Is there anything else I can get you?' David Taylor replaced the glass and resumed his seat. He wished he knew why she was so upset, and what she meant by her reference to the weekend. After a while he said, prompting, 'About the van?'

'Oh yes. You want to know when.' Jean Aubyn brushed her cheeks with the back of her hand, as if wiping away tears. 'Two or three times on odd days, over a period of three or four weeks. I can't be more specific than that. I've not seen it for a while. The last time I really remember—' She stopped, then resolutely went on. 'It was the Tuesday Tom Cheryl had that car crash. I was expecting him and kept looking out of the window, and there the damn thing was, in the mews where it shouldn't have been. It was there most of the day. But why?'

'I don't know, Mrs Aubyn,' David Taylor said. He wasn't going to tell her the possibility that had passed through his mind—that on that particular Tuesday Mr North, alias Roberts, might have been waiting to see if

Tom Cheryl did turn up as usual, or if he'd had an arranged accident and been hurt or killed. He sighed. He wished he could make up his mind which of the Cheryls had been the intended victim, or if the murderer just didn't care. 'I suppose you never caught sight of the driver.'

'Only as a vague figure, I'm afraid.'

'Well, let's forget the van for the moment, Mrs Aubyn. I'm sorry, but I need to ask you some rather personal questions.'

'You mean about Tom Cheryl. We've been lovers for years, Chief Inspector. Is that what you wanted to know? It was an—an arrangement that hurt no one, and brought a great deal of happiness to him and to me.'

'Did you ever consider marriage?'

'Of course. We're only human. But it wasn't— isn't—practical.'

'Why not? The divorce laws are pretty liberal these days.'

'Yes, aren't they?'

It was a polite, noncommittal response, and after it there was a lengthening silence. Jean Aubyn seemed lost in thought. David Taylor waited, and in the background Sergeant Drew gave an encouraging cough.

'Why not, Mrs Aubyn?' David asked again. 'The Cheryl daughters are adults. I suppose Aileen Cheryl could have fought it, but—'

'That's just it. She might have done. She probably would. I only met her once, at a party Jill gave, but Tom says . . .' The words spilled over each other, but there was surprisingly little bitterness. 'We daren't have risked it,' Jean Aubyn concluded. 'The publicity. It would have been in all the papers.'

David Taylor contained his irritation. He glanced curiously at Jean. He said, 'I'm sorry, but I'm still not clear, Mrs Aubyn. Of course divorce can be an unpleasant, messy business, even today. But it's never more than a passing wonder in the media; that would surely be a small price to pay, in the circumstances. And, if you don't mind my saying so, neither you nor Major Cheryl are very well known. Nor do you strike me as the sort of people who'd be overly sensitive to others' opinions.'

'That's not quite the point, Chief Inspector.' Jean paused. Then, 'Do either of you remember Bradford Aubyn?'

The name stirred a long-forgotten memory in David Taylor's mind. Bradford Aubyn? Some kind of popular hero when he was a boy at school. A sportsman? No. An actor? A film star?

There was no need for him to rack his brain further, for Sergeant Drew suddenly said, 'Yes, I remember him, Mrs Aubyn. He was a test pilot — about the most famous British test pilot since World War Two. He was almost a symbol of the modern British aircraft industry. He held all kinds of records — speed, altitude — and he got every sort of award. Then there was an — an accident, wasn't there?'

The explanation had really been for the Chief Inspector's benefit, and David Taylor, watching Jean, saw her wince at the word 'accident'. She was pale under her tan, and he hoped she wasn't going to break down. He wished he had brought a woman police officer with them.

But Jean Aubyn had herself under control. In a low voice she said, 'Yes, there was an accident. It was like this. Brad was very keen that I should learn to fly. He started giving me lessons as soon as we came back from our honeymoon. Unfortunately I wasn't much good at it. I had no feel for a plane. Oh, I was all right in the air — anyone is — but I just couldn't judge landing heights and distances. Brad was a fine instructor, but in the end

I think he felt I had to be forced to make a big effort. Anyway, one day we were up in a light dual-control trainer, and Brad said, "Okay, I'm taking my hands off. You're all lined up. Go ahead and land her. I won't touch a thing." '

Jean Aubyn paused for breath. She had been speaking very rapidly. She wanted only to be done with the story.

'Of course, I crashed the plane. Spectacularly, I was told later. Brad tried to save us, but it was too late, and I was sort of frozen to the controls. I spent two weeks in hospital—broken ribs, broken wrist, shock. But when I recovered I was as good as new. Brad—' She swallowed hard. 'Brad was a wreck. He'd broken almost everything he could. He's still a wreck, paralysed from the chest down, but his mind's clear. He knows what's going on, and he reads books—and newspapers.' She turned fiercely on the two detectives. 'I'd never, never divorce Brad. How could I? I've hurt him too much already. And Tom couldn't try for a divorce either, if his wife was likely to fight it, or cause any sort of scandal involving me. Brad would be sure to get to know of it. Tom understood that. Divorce was out. It always has been, for both of us. We both had to keep up a façade.'

Again, there was a silence. Jean looked directly at the Chief Inspector, and added slowly, 'I know it's a brutal thing to say, but even Aileen's death hasn't helped us. One death or divorce is no good without the other.'

And how, thought David Taylor, does one follow that? What can I say that won't sound either offensive or patronizing? Fleetingly he thought of his own wife. If she had not been killed outright, only maimed . . . But somehow he couldn't picture her easily, and he caught himself thinking instead of Jill Cheryl.

'Thank you for being so frank with us, Mrs Aubyn,' he said finally, getting to his feet. 'We're most grateful for your cooperation.'

'Yes, but what are you going to do about it? Chief Inspector, it's more important now than it's ever been that my husband shouldn't learn about Tom and me.' Jean's hands were clenched and her knuckles white. 'This weekend the doctors told me they want him to have an operation. His conditions's been deteriorating recently. And he's got to feel I'm one hundred per cent with him. Do you understand?'

David Taylor nodded. 'Yes, Mrs Aubyn, of course I understand. We'll be very discreet. I'll have to inform my superior of what you've told me, but if he agrees I can't see why that shouldn't be the end of the matter.'

'Thank you,' Jean said. 'Thank you very much.'

'We'll get her story checked?' Sergeant Drew said as he and David Taylor made their way out of the mews towards their car.

It was half a question, half a statement, and the Chief Inspector raised an eyebrow. 'Naturally, though I should be very surprised if it weren't the truth, wouldn't you?'

'I would indeed. Poor woman.' The sergeant shook his head in sympathy. 'You know, I remember more and more about Bradford Aubyn—it must have been in 1957 or '58—'

But David Taylor wasn't listening to the sergeant's reminiscences. The important thing was that the murder motive tacitly ascribed to Major Cheryl by Mrs Dawlish had ceased to have much meaning. As Jean Aubyn had implied, the Major had no hope of marrying her even with his wife dead, so he had no credible reason to kill his wife, not after all these years of acceptance. It was as simple as that. It seemed unlikely that he'd suddenly, and for no apparent reason, decided he couldn't stand her any longer. And besides, there were the threatening advertisements, followed by the various incidents, some of which had been at least partially substantiated. Further in the background was the shadowy presence of Philip North or Trevor Roberts, or whatever his real name might be.

The Chief would have to agree that, taken together, these points suggested there was no credible case against the Major. David Taylor's spirits lifted. He could phone Jill with a clear conscience and make a date with her.

'What?' he said. 'Sorry, Brian, I was wool-gathering.'

'I said, shall we call in at the local station and check out this van that Mrs Aubyn saw in the mews? Make sure it's the one those kids saw in Farlingham?'

David Taylor wrenched his thoughts back to the present. 'Sure. Okay. Let's do that. You go in alone, and be as quick as you can. I want to catch the Chief before he leaves for the day.'

But Chief Superintendent Harris had left early, and when David Taylor called Jill later in the evening, a man answered the phone. The Chief Inspector put down the receiver without speaking.

CHAPTER 14

The next morning Chief Inspector Taylor woke with a dull, grinding headache. A solitary meal in his flat, thoughts of the past, disappointment with the present, doubts about the future, all had combined to make him drink too much liquor—a rare occurrence for him. As a result he cut himself rather badly while shaving, couldn't face any breakfast except for a cup of black coffee, and went to the Yard in a bitter mood. He had deliberated about calling Jill, but had decided against it. He couldn't bear the thought of the same male voice answering her phone this morning.

Chief Superintendent Harris was not in the best of

moods either. There had been a big raid in Hatton Garden during the night, half a million pounds' worth of diamonds stolen in one of those elaborately planned operations which always led to amused reporting by the media, to the police's discomfiture. And, as usual, he was short of manpower. He found it difficult to show great interest in this business of the Cheryls, which seemed to be making little or no progress. Indeed, he had thought of taking Taylor off the case and assigning another officer to it, to try to get some new angles. But at last things were moving, if only negatively.

'Right,' he said flatly. 'I agree. We forget Major Cheryl as a suspect, at least for the moment. Concentrate on the van and this chap Roberts, North, or whatever he calls himself — if there really is only one of him. But don't let's ignore Lindsay & Beckett completely. I can't help feeling there might be some connection other than mere happenstance. Okay?'

'Yes, sir.'

The Chief Superintendent looked purposefully at his in-tray. The conference, brief as it had been, was clearly over. David Taylor retreated to his own office, where Sergeant Drew was waiting for him.

'Bit of good news,' the sergeant said at once, before David had time to close his door. 'We've got a trace on that grey van. One of our chaps out Camden Town way thought he remembered seeing a van answering the description, and he asked around. He's come up with a fellow called Couchman, who runs a newsagents-cum-tobacconists and owns a bit of property in the area — a small warehouse and a row of lock-up garages. Recently he rented a garage to a guy who gave his name as — guess what — '

'I'm in no mood for guessing this morning,' David Taylor said curtly. 'Get on with it.'

'Sorry, sir.' The sergeant's broad grin faded. 'Roberts.

Trevor Roberts. Remember—the chap that bought the van in Reading.'

'I remember all right. I suppose we might have expected something like this. Okay. We'll go and visit Couchman. Have we anything on him?' David Taylor smothered a yawn.

'A bit of form. He was charged with allowing his warehouse to be used for the storage of stolen goods. It was open and shut—he knew they were stolen all right—but he got off with a suspended sentence. Since when,' the sergeant added, 'he's always been very cooperative with the police, though the local boys say they wouldn't trust him far.'

'Let's hope he can produce a good description of our man.'

With a despairing glance at the paperwork waiting on his desk David Taylor led the way from his office. He didn't feel particularly hopeful. His head ached more than ever, in spite of the pain-killers he had taken, and even the Chief's ready agreement about Major Cheryl's status in the investigation had done little to cheer him. Nor was the slut of a woman behind the counter in Couchman's shop very encouraging. It was with great reluctance that she agreed to go and find the owner.

Mr Couchman, however, was eager to be helpful. He was a small man with a big nose and close-set eyes. His story was quite simple. Nearly twelve weeks ago he had advertised a lock-up garage for rent in one of the evening papers. A man called Trevor Roberts had phoned, inspected it and taken it for three months, paying the full rent in advance. Two weeks ago, Roberts had brought the key back, saying he'd got no more use for the place, as he'd got a new job up north. There was one funny thing—when Couchman had first called him 'Mr Roberts', he'd seemed a little surprised. Couchman's suspicions had been aroused, and he'd hastened round to the garage, which was in a nearby back street. But it was empty and clean and everything appeared to be in order.

'And have you rented it since?' asked the Chief Inspector at once.

'No,' said Couchman, 'it's still empty. I haven't got around to advertising it again.'

'Good,' said Taylor. 'You'll have to take us round there in a minute. In the meantime, give us a description of this Trevor Roberts.'

'About your height, thin, very pale hair — almost straw-coloured, if you know what I mean — and bright blue eyes.'

'I know what you mean all right,' said Taylor. 'We might think about getting you to come down to the Yard, and try for an Identikit picture.' He thought for a moment. 'And how do you know the garage was used for a grey van?'

Couchman looked about slightly uneasily. Finally he said, 'Well, you know I had a bit of trouble a couple of years ago. They used my warehouse. I didn't know a thing about it, but —'

'Yes, we know,' said the Chief Inspector wearily. 'So —'

'Well, ever since then, I've kept a sharp eye on the places I rent.'

'You mean you've got duplicate keys and you go and look round when your tenants aren't there?'

'Nothing wrong with that, is there? I'm responsible. Suppose there was a fire or something.'

'All right,' said Taylor. 'All right. Don't get worried. What did you see in Roberts' garage?'

'The grey van. I made a note of the number. And the number of the motor-bike he kept in the back of it.'

'Did he now?' said Taylor. 'Anything else, when you looked inside?'

'Yes. Black leathers — you, know, sort of motor-bike gear — and a yellow crash helmet on the front seat. And in the back with the bike was a kind of triangular wooden thing—a ramp. I suppose he used it to get the bike in and out of the van.'

'Fine,' said Taylor. 'You've been very helpful, Mr Couchman. Now you can take us round there. We'll need the key for the rest of the day.' To Drew he added, 'Get a team up to go over the place thoroughly as soon as possible. In the meantime, we'll have a quick look round.'

'Well, what do you think?' David Taylor asked the sergeant as they drove back to the Yard.

'One thing. I'd be prepared to bet that our assumption that Roberts and North are the same chap is true,' Drew said. 'It would mean he's a bit of an actor, but it's easy enough to dye your hair, and Bell-Smith couldn't remember the colour of North's eyes.'

'No.' David Taylor was thoughtful. 'You know, it could be coincidence, but that phrase Couchman used—pale hair and bright blue eyes—it reminded me of the description the Major gave of the young man who saved him from going under that bus in Oxford. I wonder . . . He never came forward when we asked for witnesses. For someone with quick reactions it wouldn't be hard to push, and then grab to prevent the accident, but give the Major a real scare.'

Sergeant Drew gave a low whistle. 'He's a cunning bastard, whoever he is, and thorough. He obviously planned the whole caper with extraordinary care, though why he should go to all this trouble defeats me.'

'It defeats me too,' David Taylor admitted. 'What's more, I've got a nasty feeling we've a long way to go before we find an answer.' If we ever do, he added gloomily to himself.

It was after eight o'clock when Chief Inspector Taylor got back to his flat that evening. The afternoon had been disappointing, though the grey van had been found at last. It was in the long-term car park at Heathrow airport. It had been there for some time, and was covered with dust. But if it was dirty outside, it was as clean as a whistle within. There wasn't a print to be found. Even places an average person might well have missed had been scrupulously polished, and smudges on the controls suggested that gloves had carefully been worn by the driver on its last trip. Couchman's garage, too, had been left unnaturally clean; the only prints to be found were Couchman's own. Sergeant Drew had been right to say they were dealing with a thorough man. Of course, his very thoroughness was suggestive.

But of what, exactly? thought David Taylor. And what do we do now? Wait for something else to turn up? Take the Chief's advice and try Lindsay & Beckett again? Go back to Farlingham? Do more research on the Major's past in the hope of coming up with a forgotten enemy? David heaved a sigh. None of these courses seemed likely to be fruitful.

He decided to stop flogging his brain. He had had no breakfast, and only sandwiches for lunch. He was hungry, but he was also tired. It was a temptation to open a can of soup and settle for that, perhaps with some bread and cheese, but he knew he needed a proper meal. Reluctantly he searched the refrigerator. There was a steak in the freezer compartment, and some peas. While they cooked, he allowed himself a beer. At least his headache had gone.

It was almost ten by the time he had finished eating. Twice in the course of the evening he had thought of phoning Jill Cheryl. Once he had gone so far as to dial her number, but he had put the receiver down before the bell started to ring. Finally, reproaching himself for his hesitation, he lifted the phone.

'Jill?'

'Yes.'

'David Taylor here. I hope I'm not disturbing you.'

'Not particularly.'

Jill heard her own iciness, and guessed how it would sound at the other end of the line. But her father had telephoned her early that morning, and asked her to make sure Jean was all right. Luckily her first period at school had been a free one, and she had found Jean in reasonable spirits. But she still blamed David for his intervention.

'I—I wanted to say how sorry I was to have missed seeing you on Saturday and—'

'Not to worry. I gather you were extremely busy with other people's affairs.'

'Yes, I—' he began, then the implication of her words hit him. 'Jill, for heaven's sake, I've got a job to do.'

'But it's not a very nice one, is it? Hounding people like my father and Jean Aubyn. Decent, good people. If they weren't, they'd have walked out on their obligations years ago.' Jill was working herself into a rage. 'Who do you think pays to keep Bradford Aubyn in that expensive nursing home, if it isn't Dad? Jean couldn't afford it by herself.'

'Jill, please!' David Taylor wasn't used to pleading with women. 'I've not been hounding them. That's not fair. I spent at least part of the weekend discovering who was persecuting your father with anonymous letters and phone calls, and I've put a stop to all that.'

'Who was it? Was it that Dawlish woman?'

'No, it wasn't.' There was silence at the other end, and David seized his chance. 'Jill, an awful lot has been happening that you don't know. Can't we meet and I'll tell you about it? It's impossible on the phone.'

'Yes. All right,' Jill said reluctantly. 'When?'

'Tomorrow I'll be in court most of the day—'

'I've a date tomorrow night.'

David suppressed a sudden twinge of jealousy. 'What

about Thursday then? Dinner?'

'Not dinner. I'll have a pile of tests to correct.' Jill hesitated. 'Why don't you come round here when you've finished with work, and I'll give you a drink?'

'Okay!'

David Taylor put down the receiver. It wasn't really satisfactory, but it was better than nothing. At least he would be able to see her and talk to her. It would be up to him to win her sympathy, to make her realize he was doing what was best for her father, for Jean, for herself. Because until the real murderer was found, the Major would remain under some suspicion, from his friends and acquaintances, if not from the police.

The court proceedings took up not only the following day, but most of Thursday morning too. For the Chief Inspector, sitting and waiting, not knowing when he would be called to give evidence, it was a frustrating waste of time. But at least he was able to decide on some action he could take as soon as he was free.

After a quick lunch David Taylor collected Sergeant Drew. Taylor explained his intentions, and together they set off for Lindsay & Beckett's offices. Here they met with an instant rebuff. Mr Lindsay, Mr Beckett and all their senior staff were in conference. According to the unhelpful receptionist, Mr Lindsay had given strict instructions that they were not to be disturbed. Whatever the police might say, she intended to obey those orders.

'That's fine,' David Taylor said cheerfully. 'No need to announce us. We'll surprise them.' And, ignoring her protests, he marched past her desk and through the door that led to the stairs. Sergeant Drew followed. 'At a guess they'll be in Lindsay's room. Think you can find it, Brian?'

'First floor front, as I remember.'

A loud murmur of voices from behind a closed door

confirmed that he was right. The Chief Inspector knocked and walked in, without waiting for an answer. The conversation in the room ceased abruptly, and James Lindsay turned to the two intruders with a baleful look.

'Oh God! You again. What now?'

'We're sorry to disturb you, Mr Lindsay, Mr Beckett. You mustn't blame your receptionist downstairs. I'm afraid we overruled her. But something's come up, and we want to ask you all a few questions rather urgently.'

David Taylor smiled round the room, but the response was poor. A striking blonde gave him an appraising stare. An older woman nodded. A man grinned a little cynically. Only Gladys Lee, more unattractive than ever in some ill-fitting sludge-coloured garments, managed what might have been interpreted as a welcoming smile, and even that was a poor effort.

'Chief Inspector,' James Lindsay said, 'we've tried to be as helpful as we can, but you're not making it very easy for us. Publishing is a business. It may not seem like it to you, perhaps—' he gestured at the pleasant room, gay with the dust jackets of the books that brightened the walls—'but I assure you it is. We all have to work very hard to earn a reasonable living—and you are interrupting our work.' Lindsay sounded a little as if he had made a speech on 'Publishing as a Business' many times before, and was adapting it to the present circumstances.

'I can only apologize again,' said the Chief Inspector coolly. He had no intention of being intimidated by the publisher. 'But murder's a serious business too, and I won't keep you long. However, as I said, there are one or two urgent questions.'

'Oh, very well,' James Lindsay agreed impatiently. 'Let's get on with it. Do you want us all together, or will you see us separately?'

'This will be fine,' said Taylor. 'It'll save time to talk to you all like this.'

'Find a couple of chairs, then.' Lindsay waved his hand vaguely round the room, and Gladys Lee moved a pile of manuscripts to provide a seat for the Chief Inspector. Sergeant Drew, content to lean against a bookcase, stopped her from further effort. The questions began, many of them intentionally repetitive and similar to those asked by himself and other officers on previous visits.

There was the occasional protest, and once James Lindsay said, 'What is this? There's nothing new here, as far as I can see. We've been through all this at least twice.' But slowly the Chief Inspector's audience became suitably wrapped in boredom.

Then David Taylor said, 'Has any one of you ever heard of a man called Philip North?' There was a general shaking of heads. 'Or Trevor Roberts? Please think hard. Could they have sent you an unsolicited manuscript, perhaps? In the last year? Or even before?'

'We'd have to check to be positive,' Lindsay said. 'As you know, we record everything we receive. Gladys, would you—'

'Later,' David said quickly. For the time being, he wanted to keep them all together. 'Before we leave will do.'

'Who are these chaps, anyway?' Beckett asked.

'Only one chap, but two names,' the Chief Inspector said, smiling. 'Or at least we think so. And he may have some more aliases, for all we know. He's probably in his thirties, with very fair hair and bright blue eyes. Does that sound familiar to any of you?'

He glanced round the table casually, and shrugged in apparent resignation when all the replies were again negative. Only Sergeant Drew knew that, in spite of his seeming indifference, the Chief Inspector was watching everyone closely. Drew was concentrating too, and it didn't escape either of them that, when Taylor mentioned fair hair and blue eyes, one pair of fidgeting hands became suddenly still.

The attractive blonde said, 'You want to talk to this man?'

'Let's say we think it possible that he might be able to help us with our enquiries.' David Taylor grinned at her, and almost as a reflex action she widened her eyes at him. 'We know a few other things about him. He drives a grey van, for example. And he rides a motor-bike.' He looked round enquiringly.

There were no affirmative answers, but he returned to his questioning for a few minutes—to distract their attention, Sergeant Drew thought. Then the Chief Inspector asked to see the rest of the staff. They were brought together in Lindsay's office, and Taylor went through the motions again, without result. It was confirmed that no manuscript had been received from a Philip North or a Trevor Roberts, but he had hardly expected that.

The Chief Inspector was fairly content as they left Lindsay & Beckett. It was possible—more than possible—they had a lead. He turned to Drew. 'We'll be late again tonight, I guess, Brian,' he said.

CHAPTER 15

At six-thirty that evening Chief Inspector Taylor left the Yard. He had with him Sergeant Drew and, in uniform, Woman Police Constable Harper. He was taking no risks. He didn't want to be accused of intimidating a witness, or worse.

The traffic was heavy, but Sergeant Drew drove with his usual calm competence, and they reached Marylebone within half an hour. The outer door of the block of flats was open. There was no porter, and only a face peering from behind a net curtain suggested that anyone was interested in their visit.

Number 3 was on the ground floor at the rear of a hall that smelt faintly of cabbage. The Chief Inspector rang the bell. A full minute passed and he was about to ring again when the door was abruptly opened.

'Oh, it's you,' Gladys Lee said, her voice flat.

'Good evening, Miss Lee. May we come in?'

'Yes. I suppose so. I was just going to have my supper.'

'We'll try not to keep you long,' David Taylor said firmly. 'Sergeant Drew you've already met. This is Constable Harper.'

Gladys Lee acknowledged the introduction with a nod and led them into her sitting-room. It was small and cheaply furnished, but its poverty was disguised by an abundance of books, and there were fresh flowers on the table. The curtains hadn't yet been drawn, and through the window the view was of trees and neatly planted flowerbeds, where Westminster City Council had turned an old, disused graveyard into a little park. Not a bad place to live if you didn't have too much money, David Taylor thought, better in fact than the uncared-for flat where he lived himself.

He said, 'Miss Lee, we came to see you at your home because we felt there were some things you might prefer to discuss in private, rather than in front of your colleagues at the office.' The room seemed over-full with the four of them standing, and he motioned her to a chair. 'Do sit down, then we can sit down too.'

Gladys Lee hovered in the doorway. 'You sit. I won't be a minute. I must go into the kitchen. My supper.'

She disappeared before he could stop her and Taylor frowned. They had lost the element of surprise. But there could be other gains. Constable Harper had followed

Gladys into the kitchen, offering to help but also keeping an eye on her actions. The Chief Inspector took a quick glance round the room, and moved hurriedly towards the portable typewriter he could see standing in its case beside a small desk. Hastily he lifted it, undid the catch and looked under the lid. It was a Remington, not new but obviously in use. At once he replaced it and gave a thumbs-up sign to Sergeant Drew. It looked as if at last things were going their way.

Bright chatter from Constable Harper in the passage warned of the two girls' return, and David Taylor turned to Gladys Lee. 'Now,' he said, as soon as she was seated, 'as you know from our meeting at Lindsay & Beckett this afternoon, we are very anxious to trace this man Trevor Roberts, and I think perhaps you might help us.'

'How? To my knowledge I've never met him, or even seen him.' Gladys Lee stared blandly at the Chief Inspector, the expression in her brown eyes hidden by the thick lenses. She appeared self-possessed and slightly aggressive. Only her constant fidgeting with the ring on her engagement finger betrayed any nervousness. 'What more can I say?'

'You know someone who answers to the description of him I gave.' It was a bald statement.

'Do I?'

'Miss Lee, please, this isn't the time for games. A man in his thirties, with very fair hair and bright blue eyes. That description fits someone known to you.' Just as they had before, Gladys Lee's hands grew still. He could feel her tension—even fear. David Taylor decided to gamble. 'Your fiancé, perhaps?' he said quietly.

Gladys Lee laughed. It wasn't a very convincing laugh, but it was a brave effort. She put her head on one side, pursed her lips and pretended to consider the matter.

'Yes, Chief Inspector, I suppose you could say that was a true statement. My fiancé is thirty-six and he has light-coloured hair and his eyes are blue—like innumerable other men in England.'

David Taylor refused to share the joke. 'Not all of them have such a close connection with Lindsay & Beckett, Miss Lee, as you and Mr—'

'Brown. My fiancé's name is Paul Brown, Chief Inspector.'

'Oh yes?'

Colour dyed Gladys Lee's sallow skin. She jumped angrily to her feet and glared at Taylor. 'You've no right, no right at all, to come bursting in here and accuse Paul and me of—of—' She couldn't bring herself to use the word 'murder'.

'I've accused you of nothing, Miss Lee, and you invited us into your flat.'

'And now I'm inviting you to leave.'

'Certainly.' David Taylor stood. 'But, if you insist, I shall have to ask you to accompany me to the local police station.'

'You mean you'd have me put in gaol?'

The Chief Inspector hesitated. He was, he knew, on sticky ground. He had no real evidence against Gladys Lee, nor for that matter against Paul Brown—if indeed that was her fiancé's name—and he remembered what Jill had said about hounding innocent people. Nevertheless, Miss Lee was hiding something. He was sure of it.

'Not necessarily,' he said, 'but it's an offence to hinder the police in the performance of their duty, and we are dealing with a murder case. If you won't cooperate, I'm afraid my options are limited.' Suddenly his voice softened, and he smiled at her. 'Why not be sensible, Miss Lee? I'm not really threatening anyone with gaol, as you put it. Why should you mind answering a few questions?'

'I don't mind, but—Why me? Why pick on Paul and me?'

David Taylor shook his head. He lied glibly. 'We're not

picking on you, Miss Lee, I assure you. All your colleagues at Lindsay & Beckett and many other people connected with the case will be interviewed at their homes in due course. We just happened to start with you because you were one of the senior people, and you lived conveniently.'

'I see.' She sounded a little relieved. 'Why didn't you put it like that before, when you came in?'

'I'm sorry,' David Taylor said meekly. 'I didn't say you were the only person we were seeing. I assumed you'd realize there would be others.'

'No. I—I thought—' But she wasn't going to tell them what she'd thought. 'You better sit down again then.'

'Thanks.' David Taylor sat and stretched his legs comfortably in front of him as if it had been a social occasion. Taking their cues from him, Sergeant Drew and Constable Harper relaxed noticeably. The Chief Inspector said, 'Incidentally, while I remember, Miss Lee, we're taking a sample of typing from all the machines that people have at home. Would you object if Sergeant Drew tried yours?'

'No. Help yourself, though it won't do you much good. It's only an old portable, not an electric job.' Gladys Lee, in her relief, showed her amusement at this apparent police stupidity. 'Chief Inspector, the instructions to the newspaper about those Major Cheryl ads couldn't possibly have been typed on my Remington.'

David Taylor shrugged. 'I imagine not, but for the sake of completeness . . .'

Sergeant Drew had already put the machine on the desk and was removing its cover. 'Is it set up for anything, miss?'

'No. Do what you like.'

'Is there an odd scrap of paper I could use?'

With an irritated exclamation Gladys Lee got up and went to Sergeant Drew's help. For a minute she fussed over the typewriter, finding a piece of Lindsay & Beckett letterhead and inserting it into the machine.

'There you are, Sergeant. All yours. Or would you like me to type something for you?'

'If you would, miss. I'm sure you're better at it than I am.' Sergeant Drew glanced at the Chief Inspector. 'That all right, sir?'

'Of course,' David Taylor agreed. 'Just tell Miss Lee what we want.'

'Miss, if you'd type: "Major and Mrs T.H.W. Cheryl, Spring Grove, Stafford Road, Farlingham, Oxon." '

Even as the sergeant spoke, Gladys Lee began to type, but almost at once she stopped. 'Is this some sort of trick?' she said angrily. 'Because if it is, I—'

'No, no, miss.' Sergeant Drew hastened to reassure her. 'Nothing like that.'

'All right.'

Gladys Lee resumed her typing, banging the keys with unnecessary vigour. Sergeant Drew, a kind, almost fatherly figure, stood beside her. David Taylor watched them. He could feel his excitement rising. If the label on the bomb parcel had been typed on this machine, they were a long step nearer to Philip North, Trevor Roberts, Paul Brown or whatever his true name might be. Bell-Smith might have difficulty in identifying him, but Couchman certainly wouldn't. And the tie-in with Lindsay & Beckett was obvious.

So it came back to Gladys Lee. Clearly she wanted to protect this Paul Brown, which wasn't unreasonable in the circumstances. But how far would she go, if confronted with real evidence? How far had she already gone to help him? She was an intelligent girl, and had jumped on the point about the typewriter—but it was the wrong point. The ease with which she had been persuaded to type the Cheryls' address didn't suggest guilty knowledge; her reaction would presumably have been different if she understood the significance of a Remington portable. Momentarily David Taylor wondered if it had been a mistake not to follow that lead earlier, but there had been so many possible machines and nothing to implicate Gladys Lee's. Anyway it had been an agreed policy at the time.

The rasp of the paper being withdrawn from the typewriter put an end to the Chief Inspector's musing. He took a photocopy of the bomb parcel label from his wallet, and produced a small folding magnifying glass. Sergeant Drew handed him the address that Gladys Lee had just typed. Heart thumping, he compared the two samples. Then, without speaking, he passed them and the glass to the sergeant.

'What is this?' Gladys Lee protested. 'What are you doing? Playing at Sherlock Holmes?'

David Taylor ignored her. 'You agree?' he said to Sergeant Drew.

'Yes, sir. Same type. Both the capital "O's" are askew and there's a little nick out of the tail of the small "g". I think there are other points too.'

'What is this?' Gladys Lee said again, her voice sharp. 'What are you playing at?'

'We're not playing, unhappily, Miss Lee.' The Chief Inspector's voice was grave. 'We believe these two addresses were typed on the same machine, your Remington over there. Of course, the comparison will have to be made with the original and by experts. But I must tell you I don't think there's much doubt. Perhaps you'd like to have a look for yourself.'

Automatically Gladys Lee took the photocopy and the piece of Lindsay & Beckett letterhead and the magnifying glass. She peered through the glass, comparing letter with letter. She seemed to take an inordinate amount of time, but at last she passed the papers and the glass back to the Chief Inspector. She cleared her throat.

'They look the same to me, I admit,' she said, 'but I don't understand. I've never — Where did you get that first one?'

'It's a photocopy of the label that was on the parcel that killed Mrs Aileen Cheryl,' David Taylor said quietly.

The blood drained from Gladys Lee's face. She swallowed several times, but no words came. Sergeant Drew helped her to a chair, and Constable Harper went quickly to the kitchen to find a glass of water. Gladys was unaware of them.

'I don't believe it. It can't be. It's not possible.'

It was no more than a whisper, and David Taylor had to lean forward to hear what she was saying. 'Miss Lee, I'm afraid you're going to have to accept it. That label was typed on your typewriter.'

'Oh no!' Gladys Lee took a gulp of the water that Constable Harper was holding for her, and it seemed to give her courage. 'You're wrong. You must be wrong, Chief Inspector. I never did it. And I'd swear Paul never did it. He'd never hurt anyone. He's a dear, kind, thoughtful man. Why should he want to kill this Mrs Cheryl?'

'I don't know, Miss Lee. Not yet.'

Gladys Lee didn't seem to hear him. 'Someone must have broken in when I wasn't here and used the typewriter,' she said, more to herself than to anyone else.

David Taylor looked at her pityingly. This was not a part of his job he enjoyed. But he knew from experience that it would be best for everyone, including Gladys Lee herself, if she broke down now. There was no point in prolonging the agony.

Making his voice sound harsh and formal, he said, 'Miss Lee, that suggestion's absurd, and you know it. Why don't you admit it? You believe — as I do — that your fiancé, a man known as Paul Brown, is in some way responsible.' And when she didn't answer, he added, 'Well, don't you?'

'Yes! Yes!' Gladys Lee's voice rose hysterically. 'I believe you. God help me, I believe it!' And knocking aside the glass of water that Constable Harper was once again holding out, she buried her face in her hands and began to sob.

CHAPTER 16

It was always the same, thought Chief Inspector Taylor. Unless they were real professional villains, when they broke, they broke completely.

It took some time for Gladys Lee to recover from her hysteria. Drew had found the remains of a bottle of whisky in a cupboard, and a strong slug of this calmed her. Now she sat, facing David Taylor, apparently oblivious of the presence of the sergeant and the constable. Having accepted the situation, she seemed, in some curious fashion, almost anxious to make amends by telling her story as quickly and in as much detail as she could.

She started to talk, in fact, before David Taylor had time to consider whether or not he should caution her. In any case, he decided, better not. It might remind her of the realities of courts and murder charges, and stop the flow of words. He felt convinced she temporarily saw her involvement with the man she called Paul Brown as part of one of the novels she edited. Maybe it was better that way.

As the Chief Inspector had half-expected, Paul Brown had picked her up. He had done it very neatly. It was nine weeks almost to the day since Gladys Lee was hurrying to the tube station after leaving her office, and a young man had held out a wallet to her, saying he had seen her drop it. She'd denied all knowledge of it, but responded by suggesting they should look inside. There was a little money—a five-pound note and two one-pound notes— but nothing to indicate the name of the owner. There weren't even any credit cards, and Paul Brown—as she came to know him—had pointed out that this was odd.

'I told him to take it to the police,' Gladys Lee said, 'but he thought you'd just put it in your kitty—I remember his very words. Then he suggested we spend it together on a drink in a pub. There was one about fifty yards along the road.'

Gladys Lee flushed. 'He was attractive—he had a charming smile.' She paused and looked round the room. 'And I don't have many boy-friends, I suppose. Anyway, we had a drink, and I told him about my job and where I lived. He was a teacher in a boys' prep school, on holiday.'

Taylor said quickly, 'Did he say which school?'

'No, I don't think he did. That was partly the point. He didn't like it, and he was looking for a new post. That's why he was always going for interviews.'

'Was he now?' said David Taylor. 'We'll go into that in a minute. What happened after you'd had a drink together?'

'Nothing. He saw me to the tube, and said he'd phone me the next day—it was a Saturday—but he didn't, not until late in the evening. I thought he . . .' She stopped suddenly.

. . . wouldn't phone, but he did, after I'd waited eagerly all day, finished David Taylor silently.

'He wanted me to meet him for lunch on the Sunday, but I said he must come here, and he did, and we spent the afternoon . . .' Again she stopped speaking. Her cheeks went red, and she stared unseeingly out of the window.

In bed, thought Sergeant Drew. David Taylor said, 'Yes, I understand. And then?'

Gladys Lee looked at him a little defiantly. 'He was wasting money in a hotel, and I invited him to come and stay here.'

All three of the police officers raised their heads. The same point had occurred to each of them. Christ! And people wonder how girls get themselves killed. Nice girls. Not tarts. Gladys Lee must have been out of her mind—or very lonely.

Paul Brown had stayed with her for seven weeks, and had left for Australia the day before Aileen Cheryl's funeral. When he left, they were engaged—hence the gold and turquoise ring she was wearing. 'It was his mother's,' said Gladys Lee. 'He wanted me to have it. I was to join him in a few months. I'm—I was—waiting to hear.'

That was the broad outline of her tale. As old as sin, thought the Chief Inspector, but as modern as today. Aloud, he said, 'I see, Miss Lee, that's all very clear. Now do you mind if I ask you a few questions?'

Gladys Lee shook her head dumbly. It seemed as if she was beginning to appreciate the full meaning of the evening's events. 'But I won't be hearing from him, will I?' she said rather piteously.

'I think probably not. That is, if we're right, Miss Lee. It's better to face the fact. The only thing you can do is answer all our questions as fully as possible. I'm sure you understand that.'

Gladys Lee nodded.

David Taylor said, 'Look, before we go any further, would you like some tea or some coffee? I know I would, and Constable Harper's very good at finding her way round strange kitchens.' He smiled at her reassuringly.

Gladys nodded again. Domestic details served to distract her a little. She turned to the uniformed woman.

'It's not very tidy, I'm afraid. And my supper! Oh, what does it matter? I couldn't eat, not now. Everything's in the cupboard by the stove, and—and I think there are enough clean cups.'

'Don't worry, Miss Lee,' said Constable Harper. 'I'll find what we want.'

'Now,' said David Taylor, 'the first questions are about Paul Brown himself. We know he had pale hair and blue eyes. How else would you describe him?'

'He was thirty-six, I know,' she paused, 'or that's what he said. He was as tall as you, and thin—too thin, I thought sometimes.' She stopped again and added, once more a little defiantly, 'It was particularly noticeable when he had no clothes on—how thin he was, I mean.' She went on quickly. 'I told him he ought to put on weight. His face was thin, too, but kind and—and nice.'

'What about his voice? Did you notice anything distinctive about it?' David Taylor asked quickly to cover her embarrassment.

'Oh yes. He had a very slight, vaguely north country accent. He was born in Yorkshire. It was a kind of bond, because I come from Lancashire. We used to laugh about the Wars of the Roses. His father was killed just before he was due to go up to Cambridge, so he couldn't. His mother had been an invalid since his father's death. He'd got her into a nursing home quite near his school, which is why he hadn't tried to move sooner. But she'd died recently. He was involved with lawyers about her estate. That was another reason why he had to go away. I hated it when he was away,' she added, suddenly completely candid.

For a moment it looked as if she would burst into tears again, but Constable Harper chose that moment to reappear with a tray. It was the tea which distracted Gladys Lee this time.

'Miss Lee, you must tell me about these trips of Paul

Brown's. They could be rather important. You said he went away for interviews and to see his mother's lawyer. Can you remember the dates he wasn't here?'

'Yes, I can, as a matter of fact.' Gladys Lee looked round the room, then stood up and fetched her plastic shoulder bag from a table by the hall door. 'I don't keep a proper diary—I never have. But I've always had a sort of engagement book—you know, to put important things in—like when Paul said he'd be back—and—and so on,' she finished lamely.

'Did Paul Brown know you were keeping these notes?' asked the Chief Inspector quickly.

Gladys Lee stared at him. 'I see what you mean, or I think I do,' she said slowly. 'No. There was no reason for him to know. I didn't mention my book. It's kind of—private. And it wasn't really notes on him. It was to remind me—like—like any engagement book.'

'I see,' said David Taylor. 'Anyway, it's fine that you kept it. Let's start at the beginning. When was the first time he went away?'

'The weekend after he came to live here. He had an interview at some posh Scottish prep school near Edinburgh. He went up north on the Friday night, and came back on the Tuesday.'

'That would be the weekend before the first advertisement appeared,' said David Taylor to Drew, who nodded. 'Though I don't see that it's got any particular significance.' To Gladys, he went on, 'And the next time? What about the following Friday—that would be the day after the first advertisement appeared?'

'He wasn't away that night,' said Gladys Lee.

'But what about during the day?'

'I wouldn't know. I was at the office.'

'You didn't take any time off work while Paul Brown was with you? So he could have gone out of London for the day without your knowing?'

'Yes,' said Gladys Lee, 'except at weekends. I wanted to be with him more, but we're terribly busy just now, as Mr Lindsay said this afternoon, and I didn't think I should. I often went in late though, and I left early when I could,' she added, almost as if she were confessing — or excusing herself for — some dereliction of duty. Duty to whom? wondered David Taylor. To her office? Or to Paul Brown? In spite of her dowdy appearance, she was a complex character.

'Was he away at all the following week?' he asked.

Gladys pulled herself together, and leafed through her book. 'No, he stayed here the whole week. It wasn't till ten days later that he spent a Monday night away. It was another interview — somewhere in Essex, I think. I didn't see him from Monday morning till I got back from the office on Tuesday night.'

'The night before the car crash, when the Major heard that possible intruder,' murmured Drew, looking up from his notes.

'Yes,' said the Chief Inspector shortly. 'And . . .'

'He was only away once more, as far as I know,' said Gladys Lee. 'That was the following weekend. He went off on Friday to see his lawyer in a town in the west country near his school and the nursing home where his mother died. He said he'd be home — he called it "home" — I was so pleased.' Gladys Lee's eyes began to brim with tears again. She turned away hastily and dabbed at her face with a grubby piece of tissue. 'He said he'd be home on Saturday, but he wasn't. And he didn't phone. It was awful. I was worried. Usually he phoned every day he was away. But he was here when I got back from the office on Monday evening. Dinner was ready, and some wine, and flowers, and — and — everything. It was then he told me . . .'

'Told you what?' prompted David Taylor gently.

'It was like this. After he'd seen his lawyer on the

Saturday, he ran into someone he used to teach with somewhere. They had a drink and got talking. Paul said he was looking for a new job, and the other man said he might know of something. Anyway, he went to stay with his friend and his friend's wife in their cottage for the weekend, and they didn't have a phone. And it turned out that this friend and another man were starting a new school next term and were short of staff. Paul was sure they'd offer him a job, and they did. But there was a snag. The school was in Australia—near Melbourne.

'I was so disappointed. I said I hoped he'd be happy there. And then he gave me this.' She held up her ring. 'I remember just what he said. He said, "We're both going to be happy there. If all goes well, and there's no reason why it shouldn't, you'll be joining me in the New Year." ' She looked at the ring and repeated, 'He said it was his mother's, but he'd buy me a better one—a diamond—when we were settled. I told him I didn't want any other . . .' She paused, again staring at the window, then turned to the Chief Inspector. 'We'll never be settled now,' she said.

'Probably not,' said David Taylor briskly. 'But let's go on. You say he didn't go away again. What about the Tuesday a week later—that's the day Mrs Cheryl was killed—was he at home then?'

'I told you,' Gladys Lee said miserably. 'I wouldn't know. I was at the office. I knew you'd ask that. I was going to say I was at home with him then—sick or something—but you'd only check at the office. No. As I said, I don't know what he did during the days, except on Saturdays and Sundays.'

'And the day he left . . .'

'It was the next Monday—that's just over two weeks ago.'

'And he'd got through all the formalities in a week?'

'Yes. He said he took his passport to Australia House

and filled in innumerable forms. There were no difficulties, because he had a job to go too. He said it would be just as easy for me, as I'd be joining him to get married.'

'Yes,' said David Taylor. 'Did you go and see him off at the airport?'

'No.'

'Why not?'

'He didn't want me to. He wouldn't let me go with him,' she said rather plaintively. 'He said he hated public goodbyes. He wanted his last memory of me to be here, where we'd been so happy . . . I'm afraid I cried . . .' she finished.

'So . . .' said the Chief Inspector firmly.

'I went off to the office as usual on that Monday morning, and he went to the airport.'

'Did he leave an address?'

'No. He said he didn't know exactly where he'd be. He said he'd write as soon as he could.'

'But what about the name of his new school?'

'He wasn't sure of that. All he knew was that he'd be met at Melbourne airport—Tullamarine, I think he called it, though I'm not sure if that's the name of the airport, or the place it's at.'

'And you haven't heard from him?'

'No. No, not yet. But it's only sixteen days and . . .' She looked at her watch and stopped suddenly, as if realizing how much of herself she had revealed. She hesitated, then faced the Chief Inspector squarely. 'Yes. I've been counting the days. I suppose there's not much point in doing that anymore. I loved him, you know . . .'

How on earth can one answer that, thought David Taylor. Better leave it and go on.

'There are only a couple more questions, Miss Lee,' he said. 'The first is about transport. Did Paul Brown have a car or a van or a motor-cycle?'

'No. You asked that at the office,' Gladys Lee said at once. 'As far as I know, he didn't. He always said he was going to catch trains.'

'Fair enough. Secondly, what about Lindsay & Beckett stationery? I see you keep some in your desk here.'

'Yes. I told you, I work at home sometimes, and I type letters now and then.'

'And James Lindsay's signature? Have you any documents here signed by Mr Lindsay?'

'I was thinking of that,' Gladys Lee said quickly. 'The answer's "Yes". There are a couple of letters he wrote to me when I was applying for the job at Lindsay & Beckett. They ought to be in the desk. But what does it matter? The letter to the newspaper and the copy for the advertisements weren't typed on my old machine. You know that.'

'I agree. At least that's clear, Miss Lee. But you must admit that Paul Brown had easy access to the right paper and the right signature.'

'I suppose so,' she said wearily. Once more the full enormity of the situation seemed to overcome her. 'What happens now? Are you going to arrest me, or anything?'

David Taylor laughed. 'No. No, I don't think so, Miss Lee. But I'd be awfully grateful if you'd let Constable Harper stay with you overnight. No, no.' He held up his hand as she started to protest. 'It's not like that. We're not worried about you running away. I assure you. It's just that I'd be happier if I knew you weren't alone. Please, Miss Lee. Constable Harper's got a toothbrush in her pocket and she can easily sleep on the sofa here. And we'll arrange for someone to be with you tomorrow, if you don't want to go to your office. I expect you've realized that we'll have to send some officers round in the morning to—to examine the flat thoroughly, and look for fingerprints and things, though I somehow doubt if Paul Brown left any.'

Gladys Lee's head bowed. 'All right, do whatever you want. I'm tired, anyway. All I want is bed.'

David Taylor said, 'Miss Lee, you know you've had a shock. Are you sure you wouldn't like a sedative? We could send for your doctor, or get a police surgeon, just as you wish.'

Gladys Lee raised her head and looked at him. Suddenly she smiled. 'I'll be all right,' she said. 'I'm not that stupid, you know. Thank you for being so—so kind.'

David Taylor was nonplussed for a moment. Then he smiled too.

'Don't worry too much, Miss Lee,' he said. 'It's a good thing we've got your part of the story clear. Thank you, too.'

Gladys Lee stumbled slightly as she went towards the passage leading to her bedroom, and Constable Harper followed to put an arm round her. The Chief Inspector and the sergeant each heaved a separate sigh, and David Taylor wiped a handkerchief across his forehead.

'Congratulations, sir,' said Drew. 'I couldn't have done it better myself. I think she's in the clear, don't you?'

'I'm sure of it, Brian,' said David Taylor. 'But this Paul Brown definitely isn't. The coincidences of dates, for example—there are just too many to be chance. And the paper, and the signature. He could easily have got hold of an electric machine. The next thing's to find the bastard. We'll check, of course, but I can guess at one place we won't need to look.'

'Australia, you mean,' said Sergeant Drew.

CHAPTER 17

At eleven o'clock Jill Cheryl gave up. She put all the
neatly-corrected tests in her briefcase ready for school
next morning, undressed, made herself a cup of cocoa
and thought of bed. She didn't want to think of David
Taylor. She didn't want to admit to herself how
disappointed she was.

He had promised to come straight from his work, but
he hadn't even bothered to telephone. Whatever the
crisis, he could surely have phoned. But no. Nothing. She
couldn't pretend she had wasted her evening, but he
wouldn't have cared if she had. He had deliberately stood
her up.

'Damn him!' she said aloud, and she knew she didn't
mean it as tears pricked her eyes.

She went into the bathroom, washed and began to
clean her teeth. A loud ring of the downstairs bell made
her jump. David? Surely not as late as this. More likely the
man who lived opposite had forgotten his key and pressed
the wrong bell again. Or possibly a drunk. She spat out
the remainder of the toothpaste and ran into the hall.

'Yes. Who is it?' she said into the house phone, making
her voice sound brisk and business-like.

'Jill, it's me. David. May I come up?'

'Of course.' Her finger was already on the button that
released the outer door.

There was no time to do anything about her
appearance and, giggling to herself, she thought how
lucky it was that she didn't put her hair in curlers at
night, or plaster her face with creams. Then, before she
expected him, David Taylor was at the door.

'Jill, I'm sorry to be so late.' He had run up the stairs

rather than wait for the lift. He couldn't admit he'd forgotten to phone, so he said, 'I just wasn't able to get away. And by the time I could phone it seemed pointless.'

'That's all right. If you'd come earlier I wouldn't have got my test papers corrected.'

David Taylor smiled wanly. He felt tired and slightly light-headed from lack of food. He was grateful to Jill for being so welcoming.

He said, 'I've had a pretty successful evening too, though not exactly pleasant. And I'm pooped. Can I have a drink?'

Jill gave him a long, hard look. His smile hid the downward droop of his mouth, but not the other lines on his face, and in the hall light his complexion had a greyish tinge. He really was dog-tired—mentally, she guessed, as much as physically.

'David, when did you last have a hot meal?'

He showed his surprise. 'Can't remember. I seem to have been living on sandwiches the last few days, most of them stale.'

'Right. You'll find a bottle of whisky on the side table in the sitting-room. Help yourself, then come into the kitchen. I've got some soup left over from supper, and I'll make you an omelette.'

David Taylor didn't argue. If Jill Cheryl was prepared to cosset him he was happy. At the moment he could think of nothing he would like more. He poured himself a whisky, drank it neat, poured himself another, added soda and took it into the kitchen. Jill already had a place laid at the table, and the soup was heating on the stove. He sat down and watched her collect the ingredients for his omelette. Suddenly he thought of the supper that Gladys Lee had prepared for herself, but never eaten.

'Poor bitch!' he said suddenly.

'What?' Startled by the exclamation Jill dropped a spoon.

'I'm sorry,' David said. 'I didn't realize I was thinking aloud.'

Jill poured a bowl of soup and put it in front of him. 'Drink this first, then tell me who the "poor bitch" is, David. Not me, I hope.'

'No, not you, Jill. Listen—'

He paused, and it was a long time before Gladys Lee's name was mentioned. Between mouthfuls of soup and omelette he found himself telling Jill he loved her. More than anything in the world he wanted to marry her. All else was forgotten.

'Will you be able to stand it? It's no joy being married to a copper,' he said a little later. 'You never know when they're coming or going. Look at tonight.'

'I'll stand it,' Jill said, her eyes bright with happiness. 'I'm pretty tough, and it can't be all bad.' She caught him looking at his watch and added quickly. 'You're not planning to go now, are you?'

'Not if I'm invited to stay,' he said. A wide grin split his face. 'And I believe I am. But I would like to telephone.'

'Is this an omen?' said Jill. 'Is this the kind of moment when the phone goes, and you leave me?'

'No, Jill, no. But I should phone now. I'll tell you in a minute.'

'It's all yours.' She waved at the instrument. 'I'll find you a robe and a razor.'

'Your last boy-friend's?'

Jill laughed. 'No. Dad's. I have a spare room and he sometimes stays here—if Jean's away, or it's not convenient.'

David Taylor made an inarticulate sound to indicate he had heard. Momentarily he considered what the Major would think of him as a future son-in-law, and what Chief Superintendent Harris might have to say about it. But he was already dialling Gladys Lee's number.

'Yes.'

The voice answered softly on the second ring, giving nothing away. He blessed Constable Harper. She was one of the most reliable and compassionate police women he knew; that was why he had asked her to accompany them tonight. He wasn't checking on her. He just wanted to be sure, for his own peace of mind, that all was well in the Marylebone flat.

He identified himself, and said, 'Everything okay?'

'Fine, sir,' the Constable answered. 'I made her a mug of hot milk, and what with that and a couple of aspirins, she's sleeping like a baby. She's really a very nice, sensible girl, sir.'

'Yes. Thank you, constable. I'll send you a relief as soon as possible in the morning. In any case, the team from the Yard will be along fairly early. In the meantime, try and get some sleep yourself.'

'Yes, sir.'

'Goodnight, then.'

'Sir, there is one thing,' Constable Harper said quickly before he could replace the receiver. 'It's about prints. You remember saying we'd be lucky if this Paul Brown had left any here. Well, when Gladys got to bed she suddenly realized she'd still got her engagement ring on. She pulled it off and asked me to put it away for her. I think she'd been wearing it all the time till now, but she didn't feel like wearing it tonight. Anyway, it had a box, probably the original one, and she's been keeping it—the box, I mean—in a plastic bag. The box is small—a proper jeweller's ring box—but it's smooth leather, and it occurred to me that Brown might just have left us a nice print on it.'

'Clever girl! He might indeed. It's just the sort of place even a careful man might forget. Well done! I'll mention it to the boys, and you tell them if you're there when they arrive.'

'Thank you, sir. Goodnight.'

'And who's that you're so pleased with?' Jill demanded as finally he rang off.

He told her then, as briefly as he could, about Gladys Lee and the man with at least three names, who had most probably caused her mother's death. 'Now we've got to find him,' he said. 'And I guess that's going to be quite a job. I shall be hideously busy in the next few days. So let's forget him for the moment, darling, and concentrate on us.'

Jill came close and put her arms around him. 'Chief Inspector, that's the best idea you've had yet,' she said.

The next morning, tired but well content, David Taylor drove to the Yard. He was wearing one of Major Cheryl's shirts, which was a size too large for him, but he didn't care. He was feeling extraordinarily happy. Not even Chief Superintendent Harris's implied stricture that he might have got on to Gladys Lee a bit sooner dampened his spirits. He took the reproof for what it was, a sign the Chief had much on his mind.

'You're sure this woman—what's her name, Lee—isn't holding out on us? She's not trying to protect her boy-friend?'

'She did at first, I think, sir, but not once she'd accepted what he'd done. It was a curious interview, as I said, but at the end she was coming clean. I'd stake my—'

'Okay. Okay. Just be sure. We want this joker caught and p.d.q. The Thames Valley people didn't call us in to sit on our fannies. There are too many unsolved cases on the books at present. The sooner you clear up this Cheryl affair, the better I'll be pleased.'

'Yes, sir,' David Taylor said meekly.

When the Chief Superintendent was in one of these moods, it was wiser to agree with him. This certainly wasn't the moment to tell him that the Chief Inspector in charge of the case intended to marry the daughter of the main protagonist, even if the Major was no longer under suspicion. The Chief wouldn't take kindly to the idea, certainly not until he'd got used to it. He'd wonder what kind of issue the media — and any defence lawyers — could make of it.

'Right then, David.' The Chief Superintendent pulled his in-tray towards him. The interview was at an end. 'Off you go, and let's hope for some quick results,' he said more affably.

David Taylor shut the door behind him and breathed deeply. He didn't believe there were going to be any quick results, not unless they had an almighty stroke of luck. Paul Brown didn't look like the kind of chap who'd be caught easily. He had shown himself to be cunning and clever; the main hope was that he'd been too clever. But it would take a lot of enquiries, checking, phone calls, shoe leather, man hours, and all that went with a big police hunt to pull him in. And, in spite of all the effort, there was no guarantee of success.

But they had to make a start. The team was already at work in Gladys Lee's flat, and he'd arranged for Gladys herself to be brought to the Yard just as soon as she was up to it. The Identikit chaps should be able to get an excellent picture from her to compare with the one that Couchman had produced. At least they would know what Paul Brown looked like — in this one of his guises, anyway.

Armed with this, the police could begin their slogging work. Australia House must be contacted, and possibly the authorities in Melbourne. Airports, ferry ports, stations, bus terminals, travel agents, hotels must all be checked. And they mustn't be misled by the Australian connection. There was no reason why any particular credence should be given to that part of Paul Brown's tale. It was equally likely he had stayed in the UK — or even in London — and assumed a new identity and appearance, or resumed an old life, content to have dealt with the Cheryls.

Motive remained a major problem; there was still no evidence about it — not enough to support the vaguest guess. More digging was necessary, Farlingham and the Major again, David Taylor decided, perhaps this time with Jill, so that there could be no question of hounding the old boy. And the Cheryls' relatives. Maybe he hadn't considered them sufficiently. Sometimes they knew more about a man than he did himself. The net would have to be spread wider.

It was Saturday before Jill was free to leave London, and by then the Chief Inspector had collected considerably more information on Gladys Lee's fiancé. The new Identikit picture of Paul Brown had proved a great success. Couchman had recognized it at once, and thought it an improvement on his own effort. Several other people remembered the flaxen-haired man with the bright blue eyes. For example, he had apparently spent a good deal of time in a café opposite Lindsay & Beckett's offices. The waitress there had thought him an out of work actor; he'd used the term 'resting' when she'd asked if he was unemployed.

Further, the motor-cycle had been traced through the licence number noted by Couchman, and the second-hand dealer who had sold it to Paul Brown had recognized his picture. More interesting was the secretarial bureau off Regent Street where Brown had spent a morning in a private office. The typewriter he'd used there was the machine on which the letter to the newspaper and the advertising copy had been produced; the date fitted, too. Finally, Bell-Smith of the Golden Hind had been almost sure he recognized his former guest, Philip North, as an older version of Paul Brown.

Unfortunately, though all this did a great deal to explain Brown's plans and methods, it did nothing to help find the man. And the rest of the evidence was almost uniformly negative. The Immigration Department at the Australian High Commission had never heard of him, nor could any official there recognize his description or his picture. The Melbourne police could trace no new or proposed private prep school in their area. There was, in fact, nothing to support the idea that Paul Brown had left the UK by sea or air—or, for that matter, that he had left London. He seemed to have departed from Gladys Lee's flat that Monday morning, and ceased to exist. Almost as a last resort, attempts were made to trace him as Philip North or Trevor Roberts, but these were equally fruitless. A great deal of work on the part of the police had brought only a succession of nil returns.

True, Constable Harper had been proved right, and slightly smudged thumb and first finger prints had been developed on the jeweller's box in Gladys Lee's flat. Some of them were Gladys's own, of course, but some were unknown. There was a strong presumption that these had been made by Paul Brown—as far as Gladys knew, no one else had handled the box—but they were not on record, and were thus of little immediate use. Gladys Lee's flat, incidentally, had been singularly clean, and bore only Gladys's prints, suggesting once again that they were dealing with a very careful villain.

'So what happens now?' Jill Cheryl asked as she and David Taylor drove down to Farlingham on Saturday.

'Oh, something will turn up,' David Taylor said firmly. 'You'll see. Our joker will have made a mistake somewhere.'

But the Chief Inspector wasn't as optimistic as he sounded. If Paul Brown, alias Trevor Roberts, alias Philip North, alias God knew who, had resumed a former identity as an established, respectable citizen, and stayed reasonably respectable for the rest of his life, the chances that he would be brought to justice seemed minimal . . .

'Don't brood, darling,' Jill said. 'We're nearly home, and if you don't look cheerful Dad will think we've had a row, and you're about to change your mind.'

David laughed. 'Maybe he'd be glad.'

'Don't be an idiot.' Jill patted him on the knee. 'You know how delighted he was when we told him on the phone.'

And, indeed, the Major couldn't have been more welcoming. He kissed Jill, shook David Taylor warmly by the hand and said, 'This is wonderful news. I'm extremely happy for you both.'

'Thank you, sir. I'm a very lucky man.'

'And Jill's a lucky girl, unless I'm much mistaken.'

They went into the study. The Major, David noticed, was still not using the sitting-room. Impulsively he said, 'Sir, Jill's told you about this chap Paul Brown, hasn't she? I mean —'

'David!'

Tom Cheryl ignored his daughter's protest. He grinned at the Chief Inspector. He liked the young man, and thought the chances were good that he would make Jill happy.

He said, 'David, you can't go on calling me "sir". It makes me feel about a hundred. Try "Tom" or, if you can't manage that right away, "Major" will do. As for the other thing, you're quite right. We can't pussyfoot around the subject, and anyway I'm curious about this Brown. We'll have a chat about him later, though I'll tell you here and now he means absolutely nothing to me. But first, I've got a bottle of champagne on ice. We've got a couple of things to drink to — you two. and my becoming a grandfather at last. John phoned a while ago to say that Celia's produced a son, and mother and child are flourishing.'

This wasn't the only piece of news that Tom Cheryl had for them. Now that the anonymous letters and phone calls had ceased—at least Bell-Smith was behaving himself, David thought—and the unpleasant rumours had died down, and he no longer felt himself being driven out of the village, he had decided to leave Farlingham. Spring Grove was up for sale.

Briefly his eyes met David's. They both knew what it was to live in a place where constant reminders of a dead woman were inescapable. 'I've got my eye on another house,' he said. 'More convenient for London, but not too far from here. After all, I don't want to lose touch with all my friends—the Galverstones, for example. If you'd care to, we could drive over this afternoon and have a look at it.'

So the weekend passed pleasantly. While Jill was at church on Sunday, the two men once again discussed the events that had led to Aileen Cheryl's death. Once again they got nowhere. The Major could add nothing to what he had already said, or to what was already known about Paul Brown. Nevertheless, David Taylor returned to London with his resolve to crack the case strengthened, if only for the sake of Tom Cheryl.

As the days passed, however, the Chief Inspector had to admit that determination and hard work were not going to be enough. Lead after lead failed. Hopes were raised, only to be dashed. Paul Brown remained elusive. Finally Chief Superintendent Harris ran out of patience.

'It's no use, David,' he said firmly. 'I've just read the latest report on the Cheryl case, and I've talked to the Commander and the ACC. You're getting nowhere. It's not good enough. We can't go on wasting manpower and money like this.'

David Taylor stayed miserably silent for a moment. He knew there was a great deal of truth in the Chief's comments. But, for both professional and personal reasons, he was loath to admit defeat.

'At least we know more or less how he did it, sir,' he said. 'With some gaps we can pretty well map his movements from the time he first stayed in Farlingham months ago.'

'Sure. Sure. I know that. I can read,' said the Chief Superintendent testily. 'But you're no nearer finding him. You don't know who he really meant to kill. You don't know the significance of those damned ads—if they were real or a blind. And you haven't a clue about motive.'

David Taylor noticed with wry amusement that, as always, it was 'you' when things were going badly, and 'we' when all was well. He said, 'I know, sir. As I see it, it's like this. If he meant to kill the Major, why did he address the bomb parcel to both of them? For a while I thought it was because he guessed that Mrs Cheryl's name on the label might make the Major less suspicious of it—less disinclined to open it. But, in that case, why deliver it on a day when he must have known Major Cheryl would be away? On the other hand, if he meant to kill Mrs Cheryl, what was the point of the ads?'

'Sure. Sure,' said Harris again. 'We've been over this ground before at least a dozen times. As far as I'm concerned, he didn't give a damn who he killed, so it didn't matter how he addressed the parcel or when he delivered it. And if that's so there's only one motive that fills the bill—revenge, plain and simple revenge. Kill the Major, or get at him through his wife. But revenge for what? God knows. You certainly don't, David . . .'

'No, sir. There's—' began David Taylor.

'What's more,' interrupted the Chief, 'now Mrs Cheryl's dead and the Major's been put through the wringer, the whole operation's stopped, so it looks as if our joker's got what he wanted. And if he's any brains at all, we won't hear from him again. Which means our chances of catching him are nil, or the next thing to it.' He looked up at the Chief Inspector with some asperity.

'What do you say to all that?'

'Yes, sir,' David Taylor agreed reluctantly. 'I guess you're right. There's absolutely nothing in Major Cheryl's past to suggest it, but I can't think of any other conceivable motive. Certainly this chap's spent a lot of time and money without any material gain that we can see.'

'And our chances? Do you agree about those too?'

'Unless he decides to surface for some reason, we don't have much hope.'

'We don't have any hope,' the Chief Superintendent replied. 'Which is why I'm taking you off the case. We'll put it into cold storage for a few weeks at least—Drew can look after the care and maintenance. You can turn your surplus energy to that damned Hatton Garden job—Superintendent Parker could do with some help.'

David Taylor sighed. 'Yes, sir. Very good.'

'So that's that,' he said later that evening to Jill, when he told her of the Chief Superintendent's decision.

'You mean the case is closed?'

'Murder cases are never closed, not until someone's been convicted.'

'But the police lose interest in them, file them away somewhere.' Jill was indignant. 'It's rotten for Dad. There'll always be people like that odious Nina Dawlish who'll believe he did it all to kill Mother.'

'I'm sorry, darling.'

'It's not your fault, David, but it's very disappointing. I was hoping so much . . .'

To change the subject, David said, 'At least the Chief took it well when I told him about us. I thought he might lecture me on confusing my private and professional lives. But no. He just said you were a very attractive girl, and I was a lucky bastard. So I am.'

For a moment Jill looked thoughtful, then she said, 'We'll ask him to the wedding.'

'Who?'

'Your Chief Superintendent, of course. David, don't you see? If we're married in Farlingham, with Dad to give me away and your Chief in the congregation, everyone, even that Dawlish woman, will have to accept that Dad's in the clear.'

'Yes,' David Taylor said softly. Then he began to laugh. 'Okay, darling, if that's the way you want it. But I'll tell you something. I'm not having Harris as my best man, and that's final.'

CHAPTER 18

The letter arrived on a mild day in mid-December. Major Cheryl always remembered the date because it was the day he moved from Farlingham to his new house. Negotiations and legal formalities had been completed in record time, and the Major saw no point in delaying his move. He was waiting for the removal van when the postman rang the bell.

'Morning, Major. Glad I caught you. There's a registered letter from America.'

'Registered?' Tom Cheryl showed mild surprise. He couldn't imagine why Celia should want to register a letter. He signed for it, and returned the postman's pen with a five pound note. 'Thanks for all your help. Have a drink on me sometime. I've put in a change of address form at the local Post Office.'

'I know, sir. We'll look after it. Thanks, Major.' The man hesitated. 'I'm sorry you're leaving us, sir. So are a lot of people in the village.'

Tom Cheryl was pleased. He smiled. 'In many ways I'm sorry myself.'

And that was the truth, he thought. He had lived here for eight years and become accustomed to the village. It had been, on the whole, a good place. Aileen had liked the house. He remembered how pleased she had been when they bought it. Poor Aileen.

The letter in his hand, Tom Cheryl went into the sitting-room. Like the rest of the house, it looked strange, unlived-in. The carpets were rolled, the pictures stacked against the walls. The china was crated. The furniture still in position had a desolate air. The Major perched himself on the corner of a packing case. Better see what Celia had to say that was important enough to register.

For the first time he glanced at the long envelope with its typed address, and stiffened. The letter was not from his daughter. Nor indeed was it from the States. The return address in the top left hand corner of the envelope was that of a firm of lawyers in King Street East, Toronto, Canada. And it was addressed to Mrs Aileen Saunders Cheryl.

The Major frowned. Maybe legal communications to a deceased person should be opened in the presence of the solicitor who had dealt with the estate. But he himself was an executor of his wife's will. What the hell? The answer was to open it.

He slit the envelope with a nail file and took out the single sheet of airmail paper. It was a fairly brief letter. Messrs Conway, Thomson and Booth regretted to inform Mrs Cheryl of the recent death in North York, Toronto, of Edward Francis Saunders, whom preliminary enquiries had suggested had been her father's brother. Messrs Conway, Thomson and Booth were seeking legal proof of this relationship because, as the late Mr Saunders's executors, they were responsible for the distribution of his estate. In his will, after bequests to various charities, he had left half the residue to Mrs Aileen Cheryl (née Saunders). This bequest could well amount to a considerable sum, and in these circumstances Mrs Cheryl would appreciate that, if she was in fact related to the late

Edward Francis Saunders, it would be in her own interest
to forward as soon as possible any supporting documents,
including birth certificates, relevant correspondence, etc.
The letter was signed, on behalf of Messrs Conway,
Thomson and Booth, by one Roy M. Conway.

The Major whistled. His first reaction was that there
must be some mistake. Certainly Aileen's maiden name
had been Saunders, but he had never heard of an Uncle
Edward Francis. As far as he knew Aileen's father had
had only one brother, who was killed in World War Two.
And what did these Canadian lawyers mean by saying
that 'preliminary enquiries had suggested' that Aileen was
the heir. What enquiries? And by whom? Private
detectives? There was something a little disturbing or
distasteful about that idea.

Poor Aileen, Tom Cheryl thought for the second time
that morning. It would be ironic if she had inherited a lot
of money, but too late. He had made her a more than
generous allowance and never queried how she spent it,
and there had been no family financial worries, at least
since his retirement from the army, but she had always
resented that she had no money of her own. She would
have liked being independent.

The doorbell interrupted his thoughts. Thrusting the
letter into his pocket the Major went to open the door to
the movers. For the next few hours he was fully occupied.
He watched his possessions being manhandled into a van,
and wondered how he had managed to acquire so many.
He walked from room to room, not saying goodbye—he
was not as sentimental as that—but making sure that
everything was as it should be.

He didn't look back as his Jaguar followed the removal
van down the drive. He had already arranged for a
woman from the village to come and clean the place
before the new owners moved in at the end of the month.
All he had to do was drop the keys off for her on his way

through the village. He felt completely detached.

The Hodgesons would be waiting for him at the new house. Everything had worked out very well. By chance Fred Hodgeson had been made redundant, and he had been able to persuade them to come and work for him, Mrs Hodgeson as cook-housekeeper and Fred as an odd job man. A flat over the garage, the use of a car to get Fred back to 'The Birds' from time to time, and the promise of other perks had done the trick easily. Farlingham, after all, was not too far away.

Then, as soon as term ended, Jill would be coming down. She had insisted. She said the house would need her feminine touch, but he knew that was an excuse. She wanted him to be happy from the beginning of his new life, not to feel lonely. Dear Jill, the Major thought fondly. David would be joining them for Christmas, and Jean for the New Year. He had a lot to be thankful for.

At his new home, Tom Cheryl found even more to occupy him. He had to decide where the furniture should be located, what unpacking should be done immediately, and what left. The need for decisions seemed never-ending, and there were plenty of other calls on his energy. It was not until the evening that he was able to relax in the room that was to be his study and sip a whisky, while Mrs Hodgeson prepared supper. A dull knocking from some part of the house indicated that Fred was taking his duties seriously.

Luckily the phone had been connected, and he was able to spend ten minutes talking to Jean Aubyn, telling her about the move, hearing how pleased the doctors were with the result of the operation, which had relieved her husband of a lot of pain, generally exchanging love and reassurances.

Finally he rang off, and suddenly remembered the letter from Toronto. He went upstairs to find it in the pocket of the jacket he had worn all day, smoothed out the sheet of paper and reread what the lawyer had written. It told him no more than it had before, but this time he noticed the date at the top of the page and realized that, as usual, it had taken more than a week for a letter to cross the Atlantic. Whatever his feelings about these lawyers and their so-called preliminary enquiries, it would be only courteous to take some action.

Mrs Hodgeson brought his supper on a tray, and while he ate he thought about what he should — or could — do. Maybe he should initiate some simple enquiries of his own before getting in touch with Toronto. At least he might try to establish if the lawyers were on the right lines.

On impulse he decided to phone Alan Saunders, a cousin of Aileen's who ran a small printing business in Reading. Tom Cheryl liked Saunders, a bluff, outspoken character, who had had little time for what he called Aileen's airs and graces. He and Tom lunched together very occasionally in London, but otherwise the families had met rarely over the years. Alan Saunders and his wife had come to Aileen's funeral, and he expressed no particular surprise at the Major's queries.

'Edward Francis Saunders, you say? No. I can't say I've ever heard of him. Who's he meant to be?'

'Aileen's uncle?'

'Uncle? You know her dad had only one brother and he was killed in the war. And he wasn't Edward Francis.'

'Are you sure, Alan?'

'Certain sure, Tom. I don't know terribly much about the family. We've never been a clannish lot. We all go our own way. But I'm positive about that.'

There was a short silence, then Alan Saunders said, 'There is one thing . . .'

'Yes, Alan?'

'Tom, I can't really remember, but there was a story about Aileen's grandfather marrying again after his first wife died. It was some kind of minor actress, I think, and he'd put her in the family way. So there must have been a child. But God knows what's happened to it.'

'I think it—he—might well have gone to Canada.'

'Canada?'

'Yes.' Tom Cheryl felt he had to offer some explanation for his interest, but he made it as brief as possible and purposely gave the impression that only a small sum of money was involved in the inheritance.

'What happens to it now she's dead?' Alan Saunders asked bluntly.

'I don't know. I suppose that's a matter for the lawyers,' said the Major. 'Their letter didn't give any details about this will.'

'I see,' said Alan Saunders. 'Pity Aileen didn't live a bit longer. Look, it's just possible we may have some papers gathering dust in the attic. At least a letter mentioning Aileen's grandfather's second marriage, or something. I'll have a good look. And let me know what happens, will you? Don't let a smart Canadian lawyer put anything over on you. What are you thinking of doing about them, anyway?'

'Well, I thought I might phone them. Maybe I'll be able to get some more information. I can always say it looks as if they may have the right Aileen Saunders, but she's dead.'

'Are you going to tell them the—the circumstances, Tom?'

'I don't know. I don't see why I should. Not on the phone, anyway. Not unless they ask. I'll see what they've got to say.'

He rang off, and looked at his watch. Toronto was surely in the same time zone as New York. Five hours back—he always remembered the phrase from Alistair Cooke's wartime broadcasts. It would be four in the afternoon there. He was quite used to phoning North America. All he needed was the Toronto area code, and that was on the lawyer's letter. He carefully dialled the fourteen figures. The wonders of science, he thought. There was a long pause, then the separated high-pitched 'burrs' of the North American ringing tone.

A Canadian girl's voice said, 'Conway, Thomson and Booth. Good afternoon.'

'Mr Conway, please.'

Another pause, then another voice. 'Mr Conway's office. Can I help you?'

'May I speak to him, please?'

'May I say who's calling?'

'Major Cheryl. I'm phoning from England. He wrote to me.'

'Oh—er—yes. I'll see if he's free, sir.'

'Roy Conway here.' Seemingly a youngish man, with almost no accent.

'You remember your letter addressed to my wife, Mrs Aileen Saunders Cheryl, as you called her.'

'Yes, indeed. What can I do for you, Mr Cheryl?'

'Your letter only arrived today, and I thought it might be simpler to talk for a minute or two.'

'Okay, sir. Yes?'

'Well, the first thing is it seems quite likely you've got the right person. I think we may be able to prove that Edward Saunders was Aileen's father's half-brother.'

'I see. Would it be possible to speak to Mrs Cheryl?'

'I'm afraid not. She's dead.'

'Oh.'

There was a pause, and the Major said, 'Look, we're on a trans-Atlantic line and this call's probably costing me a fortune. Does her death affect the situation—assuming it's the right Aileen Saunders?'

'Yes, it does. But we'll still want any documentation that's available. We'll need proof of identity. And of death,' he added. 'If there's any problem we could send someone over to see you. Or I might come myself.'

'Come yourself?' said the Major, surprised. 'Is it worth that? How much is the estate?'

'The total residue's likely to approach a million dollars, some of it property in the UK. Sir, I probably shouldn't have mentioned that figure till the situation's clearer, but it's as well to be frank, and—and it looks as if we're going to be a little dependent on your goodwill.'

'My goodwill?' said the Major. 'Why shouldn't I cooperate to the best of my ability? What happens to the inheritance now my wife's dead? Does it become part of her estate?'

'No, sir. It's not as simple as that. In fact, it's quite complex, but basically if Mrs Cheryl predeceased Mr Saunders there are other legatees. When did your wife die, Mr Cheryl?'

'About three and a half months ago.'

'In that case, she certainly predeceased Mr Saunders. It's only six weeks since he committed—' Conway stopped.

'Committed what—suicide?'

'Yes, I'm afraid so, Mr Cheryl. That was the effective verdict of the inquest.'

'Oh. Well, I'll certainly do all I can to help. I'll send over any papers I can find as soon as possible, but that may take a few days. Incidentally, who are the other legatees? Are they other relations of my late wife's?'

'Mr Cheryl, it's a little complex to talk about on the phone, and I'm not sure I should discuss it with you, not until the question of identity has been settled. I suggest you talk to your own lawyer—solicitor, you call him, don't you? He'll know the sort of thing I'm after, and you could have him send me the relevant documents. Or give me his name and address, and we'll contact him direct.'

'That would just waste time. I'll show my solicitor your letter and tell him of this phone conversation.'

'Okay, sir. It's up to you. When we've considered your

reply we'll be in touch. The main thing from our point of view is to establish the relationship and the date of your wife's death.'

'I understand. Goodbye.'

'Goodbye, sir, and thank you for calling.'

Slightly irritated, Tom Cheryl replaced his receiver. Lawyers, he knew, were not apt to be forthcoming about their clients' affairs, but in the circumstances he thought this Conway had been unnecessarily cagey. But he'd do his best. He'd arrange for the lawyers to be sent confirmation of Aileen's death, and birth certificates and anything that Alan could produce, and forget the whole thing.

Meanwhile he wouldn't mention it to anyone. He had to admit that for a few minutes his hopes had been raised. Half a million dollars was a lot of money, not only for him, but for the girls. What was it Alan had said? 'Pity Aileen didn't live a bit longer.'

He stood stock-still. Why hadn't Aileen lived a bit longer? Because she'd been murdered. And, as it turned out, others *would* profit from her death. Other what? Relations? Or institutions? They could be charities, perhaps. Though the Toronto lawyer's words had seemed to imply people.

And, even if there were such people it was irrelevant. No one could have known that Edward Francis Saunders would take his own life. Suddenly, in spite of the efficiency of the central heating in his new home, Tom Cheryl found himself shivering. His wife had died a violent death some weeks before Edward Francis had conveniently committed suicide, and because of this, a fortune was apparently up for grabs. Suppose it weren't suicide. A murderer's ideal would be to have an untimely death classed as suicide. Suppose, for once, one had succeeded. At the very least, here was a motive, and the police had put much emphasis on motive.

The Major sat staring into space. What should he do? Who to confide in? David Taylor was the obvious choice, but he was a policeman and, having been under suspicion himself so recently, the Major was not prepared to direct an official finger at someone else who could just as easily be innocent. Besides, he didn't know all the facts. He wasn't even sure that Aileen really would have been this chap Saunders's heir. He could find himself making baseless accusations against a heart research fund, or God knows what respectable institution, merely because Aileen had died when she did. It was absurd. He was letting his imagination run away with him.

Giving himself a metaphorical shake, the Major went to bed. Naturally enough he was tired after the day's efforts, and though it was his first night in a new bedroom, he went to sleep at once. He woke refreshed, but still aware of a vague uneasiness. And, in the days that followed, in spite of his preoccupations with the house, with Jill's arrival, with preparations for Christmas, the uneasiness persisted. He had consulted his own solicitor, but without voicing even the mildest suspicion. But he admitted to being curious, and he hoped that Conway, Thomson and Booth might be more forthcoming when approached by legal colleagues. To some extent, they proved to be.

Edward Francis Saunders, it appeared, had emigrated to Canada in his teens and had made a small fortune out of property development in Canada, the United States and to a lesser extent in the United Kingdom. In his will he had left the bulk of his estate to Mrs Aileen Saunders Cheryl, unless she predeceased him. If she had done so, her inheritance would pass to different legatees, unrelated to the Saunders family, and none of them in the UK.

'So that means neither Jill nor Celia will inherit anything and, more importantly, neither will that chap Paul Brown,' said the Major to David Taylor.

The two men were taking a walk. It had been a good Christmas. Tom Cheryl was happy and relaxed. The boxer puppy—a joint present from Jill and David—was pulling at its lead, and already giving him a great deal of pleasure. Plans had been made for an Easter wedding and, almost without thinking about it, he had confided in his future son-in-law.

'There's no doubt Paul Brown was British, is there?'

'I don't think so, Major. Gladys Lee said he had a very slight north country accent, but no one's ever suggested he might be a North American.'

'Too bad.' Tom Cheryl grinned ruefully. 'I hoped I'd found another suspect for you—and one with a motive for two murders. But, of course, it's far-fetched.'

David Taylor smiled, but said nothing. They had turned into a field and he bent and picked up a stick lying in the grass. He threw it for the boxer, now free of his lead, and the dog went bounding after it. There was no point in raising the Major's hopes, David thought, but undoubtedly it was an odd coincidence, and coincidences were often suspect. At least he'd look into it when he got back to London.

CHAPTER 19

Chief Inspector Taylor returned from his Christmas break to find a huge backlog of work. Crime does not cease on holidays. He had been considering whether to consult his Chief about the Toronto lawyer's letter and its implications for the Cheryl affair, but he had decided not to. He would first try a little personal investigation. After all, it was the Chief Superintendent who had taken him off the case, and Harris might well simply order him not to waste his time. It seemed that, from Harris's point of view, the Cheryl case was moribund. As a result, unless someone took some action, the Major could go through the rest of his life tinged with the stigma of suspicion. This angered David Taylor, and he had Jill to consider, too.

Fortunately, the events in Canada seemed to centre on Metropolitan Toronto, and he had a contact in the police force there. A year or so ago he had worked closely with a Toronto detective-inspector on a drugs case. They had never met in person, but Taylor had found a lot in common with Inspector Paretti.

With Jill still in the country and thus no incentive to get home to her, David Taylor worked long hours. Late one evening between Christmas and the New Year, he put through a phone call to Toronto. Luck was with him, and Paretti was in his office.

'It's good to hear from you,' said John Paretti. 'Happy New Year. I hope you're flourishing.'

'I'm fine, thanks. About to get married again.'

'Congratulations, my friend. Have you called to invite me to the wedding? Or can we do something for you?'

'John, it's like this . . .' David Taylor explained the situation briefly, emphasizing names and dates. There were a number of things he wanted to know. Was there any question about the alleged suicide of Edward Saunders? What were the exact terms of the will? Assuming that it was Aileen Cheryl who should have been the heir, who would now inherit? If the new legatee was an individual, was anything known of him, and could a description be provided?

John Paretti promised his cooperation, but Taylor added, 'Be careful, John. Don't rock any boats, and above all don't scare anyone off. This enquiry's a bit unofficial, but we'll go through the formalities if your reply looks promising.'

'I understand, David. Don't worry. I'll do a bit of legwork myself, and take care. Shall I call you back, or would a Telex be okay.'

'There's nothing against a Telex, but mark it for my attention.'

'Fine. Okay. Give me a few days. You know what things are like in the holiday season. We don't shut down for two weeks like I gather you guys over there do, but a lot of people take extra time off.'

'Yes. Great, then. And thanks a lot.' David Taylor rang off, feeling quite pleased with himself. At least he had set some wheels in motion.

The Telex from Toronto arrived early in the New Year. Paretti had done his work well. Disentangled from the telegraphese, it appeared that Edward Francis Saunders had definitely committed suicide by taking an overdose of hypnotic drugs at his house in North York, a residential suburb of Toronto, some nine weeks ago. The usual investigation had disclosed nothing to suggest foul play of any kind.

As the lawyers had said, after some small bequests to charities and a slightly larger sum to one Clive Ryder, the bulk of his estate was left to Mrs Aileen Saunders Cheryl, his closest blood relative, if she survived him. It was confirmed that the total residue was likely to be about a million dollars.

However, if Aileen predeceased Saunders, the situation was quite different. The residue of the estate would then be split in two, half to St Simon's College of the University of Toronto to build a 'Saunders Memorial Theatre', of which Ryder should be the first Director, and the other half outright to the said Clive Ryder.

Ryder, it seemed, was an Associate Professor of the University and Deputy Head of the Drama Department at St Simon's. He was in his mid-thirties, height 1.78 metres, weight 63 kilograms, hair brown, eyes hazel. He was a Canadian citizen, but not Canadian born; he had emigrated from the United Kingdom some fifteen years before. Nothing was known against him, but he had visited France and Germany on some university project during both his Easter and Summer vacations the previous year. His relationship with Saunders, whom he had met soon after his arrival in Toronto, was based on their mutual interest in drama. They had been close friends, and Ryder was a frequent visitor at Saunders's house. The will was dated over three years ago, and it was by no means impossible that Ryder could have learnt of its contents.

Further, Saunders had suffered from leukæmia, though it was in a stage of remission, and there was no indication of an imminent fatal outcome. Still, his suicide had merely hastened the inevitable; maybe he had suddenly decided to end an unendurable suspense. A letter with more detail and a copy of the will was in the mail.

Biting his nails, David Taylor waited for the letter. The Telex was at least very suggestive. The description didn't fit, but Ryder seemed to have some connection with the theatre, and an expert could do a lot to change his appearance, quite apart from simple things like hair dye and coloured contact lenses. Ryder seemed to have been in Europe at the right times, too. Could he have entered the UK unnoticed? He must check with the immigration people in the morning. Finally, there was the question of motive. The money itself provided that. On the other hand, it was hard to imagine that anyone could forecast a suicide with such precision, and kill Aileen Cheryl at just the right moment . . .

A couple of days later Paretti's letter arrived. It added little to the Telex, though what was new was significant. The Head of the Drama Department at St Simon's was elderly and on the point of retiring. Ryder, his Deputy, was an arrogant guy, not greatly liked in his college, and it had been expected that he would be passed over, and an outsider appointed to the senior job. Saunders's munificent bequest to the College, tied as it was to Ryder, could alter all this. Apart from the half-million dollars, Ryder had a career—probably a professorship with life tenure—and considerable prestige to gain from Aileen Cheryl's timely death.

In conclusion, John Paretti had written: 'On the whole, it looks as if you may be on to something, so I've been moving very, very softly, which is partly why I've been so slow. As you said, it's vital not to alert the guy to our interest. For that reason, I've not been able to get hold of a good photograph. He seems fairly camera-shy. But I enclose a group picture of his College faculty taken last year at the graduation ceremony. I've marked Ryder, and you could try a blow-up. It might be recognizable. Or how about a trip over here to identify him?'

Some hope, David Taylor thought. The Yard wasn't likely to send him to Canada; it wouldn't even be useful. It was Gladys Lee they should send, and that was not very practical. But having Paretti in Toronto was a considerable help.

The next day Jill returned to London. David Taylor had missed her more than he would have thought possible. He lost no time in outlining the latest developments to her, but insisted that she shouldn't mention them to her father for the time being.

'Jill, darling, the chap could be completely innocent,' he warned. 'We could be building the whole thing on a quicksand. Sure, we know he's got a motive of sorts, and he could have been here at the right time, but that's really all we do know.'

'What about the dates? Can't you tell if he did come to England?'

'No. It seems not. The immigration people say that no

record is kept of Commonwealth visitors if their passports
show they were born in Britain. For that matter, he could
easily have a British passport as well as a Canadian one.
Many Canadians do. The British authorities don't mind
in the least, though the Canadian aren't too keen, if they
know. And if he had a British passport, he could pass
through immigration controls totally freely, unless he was
on the Watch List.'

'The what list?'

'Oh, it's just a list the officials have at ports of entry, of
people who are wanted for one thing or another. There's
no record of a Clive Ryder—or any of his other names, if
they are his other names—on it.'

'So what we've really got to do is get him identified as
Paul Brown or one of the other characters,' Jill said.

'Yes,' said David Taylor. 'Surprisingly enough that
thought had occurred to me.' Jill looked at him quickly.
'I'm sorry, darling,' he went on. 'But it's not quite as
simple as it sounds. Anyway, I'm starting with Gladys
Lee. She's going to meet me for a drink in her lunch-hour
tomorrow. I thought it might be less intimidating than
asking her to come to the Yard again. But don't forget,
even if she does recognize him, it's not necessarily
evidence we could use. That would mean identity parades
and things of that kind.'

'I see.' Jill laughed. 'Drinks with your female
witnesses—you're not trying to make me jealous, are you,
David?'

'You haven't seen Gladys Lee,' said David. 'Or you
wouldn't talk of being jealous.'

When Gladys Lee came into the pub where he was
waiting, it took David Taylor a moment or two to
recognize her. He remembered Jill's comment, and had to
smother his amusement. For Gladys had changed. Her
hair had been cut and styled, she had lost weight, she was

wearing a new sheepskin coat over a smart green dress and she'd done her best to conceal her thick lenses with fashionable spectacle frames.

'Good morning,' he said, standing up. 'How nice you look.'

Gladys Lee smiled at him. 'Thanks to your Constable Harper,' she said. 'Betty Harper pointed out to me very clearly that I either let this—this affair overwhelm me, or I bought some new clothes, had a hair-do and faced up to it. So I decided to take her advice.'

'With smashing results.' The Chief Inspector made a mental note to have a congratulatory word with WPC Harper.

Gladys Lee gave a little nod, accepting the compliment. 'I'll tell you something else. I was dreading the idea of going back to the office. You know how things get around—I thought they'd all snigger at me, without my ring and everything. But no. Mr Lindsay and every-one have been awfully kind and sort of—interested in what's been happening.'

'Great,' said David Taylor. 'But I hope you didn't tell them too much.'

'No. Certainly not. I haven't even told Mr Lindsay the whole story.'

David Taylor went to buy drinks, and on his return produced the photographs, first the one of the whole faculty. 'Do you recognize anyone here?'

'You mean Paul Brown?'

'Yes. Any possibilities?'

Gladys Lee looked carefully at each face, and the Chief Inspector offered her his magnifying glass. She shook her head. 'No. None that I could swear to.'

David Taylor hesitated, then he produced the enlargement. 'What about this chap? Try to imagine him with fair hair and blue eyes.'

Gladys Lee remained noncommittal. 'It's such a blurry

picture,' she said. 'If I could see him in person, I'm sure I'd know. After all . . .'

I know what you were going to say, thought David Taylor. After all, he did live with me for six weeks.

'Oh well, it doesn't matter. It was a long shot,' he said aloud. 'Thank you for trying.'

Late in February, in the middle of a dull Monday afternoon, the Chief Inspector's office phone rang.

'Toronto calling, sir. It's an Inspector Paretti.'

'What? Put him through,' David Taylor said quickly. Then: 'John? How are you? What is it? Any news?'

'You could call it news. You remember the Ryder business?'

'I'll say I do.'

'Well, Ryder's coming over your way.'

'Here—to the UK?'

'Yes. Look, I've been keeping quiet tabs on the situation. Conway—the lawyer, remember—has acted pretty quickly. He's got all the courts to grant probate of Saunders's will. And it looks like Ryder's been given a week's leave of absence to go and inspect his property—his and the College's—on your side.'

'When?'

'He's got a flight booked for next week—Air Canada leaving Toronto Tuesday night, arriving London Wednesday morning.'

'This sounds like good news,' said David Taylor. 'Let me think for a moment.' He paused. 'Do you know exactly what Ryder's going to be doing?'

'No, not exactly. But Conway's legal correspondent in London—the guy Ryder's got to check in with—is a lawyer called Peregrine Blackstock. He's part of a firm located somewhere in the City of London. I've got the address here.'

'That's all right. We can find him. Ryder's still got no

idea you're — we're — interested in him?'

'None at all, as far as we know. We've been very careful.'

'Great,' said David Taylor. 'It's a chance too good to miss. We'll see what we can do here. I'll keep you informed. And thanks for everything. Thanks a lot.'

'That's okay, David. Any time. Have a good day.'

It's a chance too good to miss, repeated David Taylor to himself. He could visualize the beginnings of a simple plan. But Harris must be put in the picture at once. And I've already delayed too long, thought the Chief Inspector, as he reached for the phone. It won't be a pleasant interview.

The Chief Inspector was wrong. The interview was not unpleasant. In fact, Chief Superintendent Harris, having at last found time to glance through the circulating file of incoming Telexes for the past couple of months, had been on the point of demanding an explanation for Paretti's message. Taylor's request for a conference forestalled him, and when he heard the full story of developments in the Cheryl affair, he gave David only a mild rebuke.

'You really can't go haring off on your own like this,' he said, 'though I know you've got a personal interest in nailing someone.' He paused. 'Only make sure it's the right someone. Still, as you say, we can't miss this chance. What's the plan?'

The Chief Inspector explained. Harris nodded, and merely added, 'Don't take any risks, David. If you're sure he's our man, sew him up by all means. But it's a complex business. Make sure the case is open and shut.'

CHAPTER 20

'What you're saying, David, is that everything depends on this girl Gladys Lee, and Couchman, the garage man,' Tom Cheryl remarked. 'I'm sure I won't be able to contribute anything.'

The two Cheryls and David Taylor were dining with Jean Aubyn in her flat on Wednesday evening. Inevitably conversation had turned from the forthcoming Easter wedding to Professor Clive Ryder's appointment with his London solicitor the next morning. He had arrived on schedule, been identified as he passed through the immigration controls at Heathrow and was now under discreet police surveillance.

'It's Gladys Lee who knew him best, obviously,' said Jean. 'What happens if she can't identify him? Or, worse, denies she ever saw him before?'

'If she's positive she doesn't know him, and Couchman doesn't either, there's not much we can do. If they disagree, I don't know. That spells uncertainty, and the courts don't like uncertainties . . .' David Taylor shrugged. 'A lot depends on what happens at the time.' He was not prepared to reveal all his plans, even to the Cheryls and Jean. He had briefed his witnesses individually, and the Major only needed to know his own part.

'There's a point that's been bothering me,' said Tom Cheryl. 'How could this chap Ryder possibly have hoped to get away with it? He must have known he'd come under suspicion when Saunders died, and Aileen's name was found in the will.'

'I know. That worried me at first,' David Taylor replied. 'But I don't believe he had any idea that

Saunders would suddenly do away with himself. By the time he died naturally from his illness, the connection might well never have surfaced. Suppose you'd got that lawyer's letter in a year or two's time, Major. Would you have been suspicious enough to take any action?'

'No, probably not. But you'd have known about it, David. Jill would have told you, if I didn't.'

'Ah, but the other thing Ryder didn't know was that I was going to marry your daughter, did he? From his point of view, that was another bit of bad luck.'

'You mean our engagement's had other uses?' said Jill. 'I'm glad to hear it.'

David Taylor grinned, but he continued, intent on his exposition. 'You know, the interesting thing about this case, assuming Ryder's our man, is the number of "fall-back" positions he devised. First, the timing, so that no connection would be made between the murder and the motive. Then the advertisements and the incidents, suggesting that you, Major, were the intended victim, and Mrs Cheryl's death merely accidental.'

'One of those incidents, as you call them, damn near killed me,' said the Major. 'Remember that car crash after the wretched man had tampered with my brakes?'

'Yes,' said David Taylor. 'But we know he didn't intend the crash to be fatal, because he'd already sent further advertisements to the newspaper. Something must have gone wrong. Maybe he intended your brakes to fail sooner, on the level, and maybe he didn't allow for the appalling conditions that morning.'

'Maybe,' said the Major. 'Anyway, I suppose his next plan was that I'd be accused of the murder. He'd done his reconnaissance and watched this house, and he thought my—my friendship with Jean would give me a motive.'

'And lastly,' said David, 'if all that went wrong, we still had to find him through a mass of aliases and false identities and misdirections.'

Throughout this duologue, Jill had been silent. Suddenly she broke in. 'But if he's not recognized, will you let him go back to Canada? Just like that? Get away with murdering Mother and threatening Dad and causing God knows what unhappiness?' She was beginning to sound indignant.

'Jill!' her father protested. 'We're not certain the beggar's guilty.'

'Well, I am! The more I think about it, the more sure I am! And don't say that's female logic. Too much fits together too neatly. Quite apart from the money.'

'We need more than a motive,' David Taylor said mildly. But she's right, he thought. It's not just that I want this fellow to be guilty, for the Major's sake, for Jill's, for my own. I feel in my bones he is. But I've got to get evidence that'll stand up in court — or a confession. Tomorrow's going to be a tricky day.

The Chief Inspector had arranged matters with great care. Once Peregrine Blackstock and his partner, George Drayton, had been persuaded that they need do no more than provide opportunities for the discreet observation of a client of their Canadian associates — a client they themselves did not know personally — they were prepared to cooperate. David Taylor merely told them that an important question of identity was involved, perhaps leaving the impression that the wrong heir might be coming to call. They were thus keen that matters should be clarified, though somewhat doubtful about their involvement in the Chief Inspector's schemes.

Fortunately their suite of offices was very suitable for David Taylor's purposes. It was on the eighth floor of a modern, glass-fronted block. A receptionist sat in a spacious waiting area, expensively furnished in office modern, and with wide windows giving a fine view of the

City and St Paul's Cathedral. The partners' private offices opened off this area.

Chief Inspector Taylor, Sergeant Drew and a uniformed constable arrived early, accompanied by Major Cheryl. After introductions, Blackstock said, 'We've cancelled our appointments for the rest of the morning, as you asked, Chief Inspector. You're quite sure there'll be no trouble or scandal?'

'If there is any publicity, sir,' said David Taylor, 'it can't possibly reflect on your firm. Your only part will have been to assist the police with their enquiries. And as Officers of the Court . . .'

'All right, Chief Inspector, I know.'

'Now, gentlemen. You remember what we agreed. From your point of view, there's just one unusual aspect to this morning's proceedings—and even that's pretty normal. Mr Blackstock will try to get Mr Ryder to accept a drink or a cup of coffee—preferably a drink. And put aside any documents he handles. You know what we're after—a good set of fingerprints. I assure you we'll keep no record of them if they don't match up with some we already have.'

'Fine,' said Blackstock. 'I'm game.'

'There's one other thing I thought of overnight,' said the Chief Inspector. 'It's partly for Mr Blackstock's own protection, but I'd be happier if Sergeant Drew were close at hand during the interview with Mr Ryder—in Mr Blackstock's washroom, with the door slightly ajar, perhaps.'

'For my own protection?' said Blackstock. 'I'm not sure I like the idea, but if you put it like that . . . We can rely on your sergeant's discretion? After all, any conference with my client is confidential.'

'Absolutely, sir. You know as well as I do how difficult a complaint would make things for us.'

'Well—'

The conversation was interrupted by the arrival of Mr Couchman, the newsagent who had rented his lock-up garage to the fair-haired, blue-eyed Trevor Roberts. Mr Couchman had none of the solicitors' doubts. He knew exactly what he was meant to do, and he intended to enjoy himself doing it.

'I sit here in this waiting-room and watch people coming in. I try to make them notice me, but I behave natural-like, not too curious, not enough to frighten them. And if I recognize anyone, I don't give it away, not until they've gone through. Then I give you the word. You'll be over there.' He pointed to a corner of the reception area, where David Taylor proposed to establish himself behind a paper.

The Chief Inspector laughed. 'That's it, Mr Couchman, but don't overplay your part. If we have got the man we want, we mustn't warn him too soon. All we want you to do at this stage is shake his confidence a little—that is, if he's the right chap.'

Then Gladys Lee arrived, a little late and a trifle flurried. The same coat, David Taylor noticed, but a different dress, and she'd had her hair done for the occasion. He greeted her warmly and introduced her to the others. Gladys Lee and the Major looked at each other with interest; they had a great deal in common, in that they had both in different ways been targets of Paul Brown's attention. As planned, the two of them went with the constable to Drayton's office, leaving the door slightly open. The Chief Inspector had a final word with the receptionist.

'I know you're not quite sure what all this is about, but that's intentional. All you've got to do is behave perfectly normally. Ask anyone who arrives with an appointment to wait here, just as usual. Try not to pay any special attention to anyone.'

The girl was both attractive and intelligent. She looked

up at him brightly. 'I understand, sir. I'll do exactly as you say.'

Twenty-five minutes later—fifteen minutes after the time of Ryder's appointment—everyone was on edge. Even Mr Couchman was fidgeting. Suddenly the outer door opened and a man came in. He looked round the room with reasonable nonchalance, and gave his name softly to the receptionist. Without a tremor in her voice she said clearly, 'Oh yes. Mr Ryder. Mr Blackstock will see you in a moment. Please take a seat.' She reached for her telephone.

Ryder sat down by the windows. He was certainly in his mid-thirties, and thin, but his hair was brown and his eyes hazel, as Paretti had said. For a moment his gaze rested on Mr Couchman. As far as the Chief Inspector could see, neither gave the slightest sign of recognition, except perhaps for a minute hasty movement of Ryder's head—and that's hardly evidence, David Taylor said to himself.

Mr Blackstock himself came out to welcome his new client. 'Professor Ryder, I hope you had a good trip. We're glad to see you. Come along in.' He took the Canadian's outstretched hand, albeit a little nervously. 'Not a very nice day, is it?' he said as he ushered Ryder into his office.

'Warmer than it is at home.' The voice was pleasantly modulated, the accent mid-Atlantic. Blackstock shut his office door firmly behind them.

Couchman said at once, 'I don't know. I just don't know, and that's the truth. He's the right size and shape, but the voice is different, and the hair and the eyes.'

'Try to imagine fair hair and blue eyes, Mr Couchman,' said David urgently. Then, after a pause, 'No use?'

'I couldn't swear to him, not in court,' said Couchman.

'But I'll do what you said, if that's what you want.'

'I think I do,' said David Taylor, 'but let's hear the others.' He went into Drayton's office.

The Major shook his head firmly. 'As I said, it's no good. There was really only that time in Oxford, and I scarcely took him in.'

Gladys Lee hesitated. She said, 'Chief Inspector, I couldn't swear to him. I couldn't. He's different, even his voice, but I've got a funny feeling it is Paul. He could be. He could be,' she repeated thoughtfully. Then, more strongly, 'I'm prepared to try, too.'

David Taylor took Gladys Lee's hand in his, and felt her tautness. 'Okay,' he decided, 'we'll go ahead. Do exactly as we planned.' He returned to Couchman. 'We'll go ahead,' he repeated, 'but this time I'll wait with the others.' And pray, he added ruefully to himself as he went back to Drayton's office, leaving the door wide open.

If you wanted a cliché to describe the tension of the next half hour, thought David Taylor, it was 'palpable'. They waited, still and silent but for rapid breathing.

Suddenly Clive Ryder laughed. Blackstock had opened his office door at the end of their meeting, and made some mild joke.

For a moment the Chief Inspector was unsure if Gladys Lee was acting, as they had planned as a last resort, or whether her reaction was wholly genuine. All he knew was that she stiffened beside him. Her hand went up to her mouth. Then, 'That's Paul,' she said, in a whisper, almost to herself. 'I'd know his laugh anywhere.' She pushed past David Taylor and rushed across the reception area.

'Paul! Paul!' she cried. 'Paul, you're back! Why—' She threw her arms around him and buried her face in his shoulder.

Clive Ryder's reactions were ambiguous. Naturally

enough he clutched at the girl in his arms, and paused. Then he pushed her away roughly and turned to Blackstock. 'What is this . . . ?' he began.

On cue, Couchman rose from his armchair. 'Mr Roberts,' he said, as he'd been instructed. 'Glad to see you again. There are one or two little points about that garage . . .'

Taylor decided it was time for him to take a hand in the game, to put on the pressure, to shake Ryder's confidence, to force some revealing move. He moved forward from Drayton's office and confronted his quarry. 'Mr North, I think,' he said. 'Mr Bell-Smith of the Golden Hind in Farlingham has told me of you.'

Major Cheryl had followed the Chief Inspector and stood in the doorway, the uniformed figure of the constable behind him.

Visibly Ryder controlled himself. He turned again to Blackstock, and said casually, 'I asked, what is this?' he said. 'Some kind of British gag? Who are these people?'

At that moment Sergeant Drew appeared from Blackstock's office, a hand behind his back. Very obviously he nodded and gave a 'thumbs up' sign to Taylor. Ryder watched him, his face blank.

The Chief Inspector was now in the middle of the reception room. He took it upon himself to answer Ryder's question. 'Perhaps I should make some introductions,' he said softly, 'though they're not really necessary. First, here's Major Cheryl. You know him well—you've met him a number of times, and it was his wife's death that brought you your fortune. Remember?'

He paused. Ryder said quickly, 'Who the hell are you? Look, Blackstock, you're my lawyer over here. Do something to protect me from these maniacs.'

Before Blackstock could intervene, Taylor continued. 'You've met Major Cheryl's housekeeper, too. You delivered a special package to her some six weeks ago.

And, Mr Brown, the lady beside you is Miss Lee—surely you don't want me to introduce you to your fiancée.'

Again he paused, and Gladys Lee once more struck precisely the right note. 'Paul, Paul,' she said. 'Why didn't you write? I've been waiting . . .'

David Taylor interrupted her. 'And, Mr Roberts, the gentleman here who mentioned the garage is Mr Couchman of Camden Town. You must recall him. You left his property in excellent condition, he tells me. And you'll be glad to know your van's quite safe. We found it where you abandoned it, at Heathrow.'

He stopped and his voice changed. He had been speaking quietly and casually, as if at some kind of bizarre social occasion. Now he went on harshly. 'And the police officer behind you is Sergeant Drew. The constable in the doorway there is called Wilson. And I'm Detective Chief Inspector Taylor of the Metropolitan Police. Mr Ryder—or Brown, or North, or Roberts—I must ask you to accompany us to Scotland Yard to assist us with enquiries into the murder of Mrs Aileen Cheryl.' As the Chief Inspector uttered the formal words, the uniformed Constable Wilson moved towards Ryder.

'Why the hell should I?' said Ryder roughly, his mid-Atlantic voice replaced by a strong north country accent. 'You've got nothing on me. What can you have? Is this some kind of set-up?'

'Nothing on you, Mr Ryder? You know you've been identified—under various names—by a variety of witnesses. And we've other evidence, too.'

'Other evidence? What?' asked Ryder sharply. He corrected himself immediately. 'What do you mean? What of?'

Sergeant Drew held up a sherry glass, handling it carefully by its base in a handkerchief.

'For one thing, we've got your fingerprints on the glass you've just used, Mr Ryder,' David Taylor said. 'And you remember the leather box that held the engagement ring you gave to Miss Lee . . .'

As Ryder let his eyes stray round the room, the Chief Inspector's voice tailed away. This was the moment. There had to be some response, some words from Ryder that would serve as a confession and be admissible as evidence.

But Taylor had misjudged his man. He knew that Ryder was careful and meticulous, but he had failed to appreciate that for a supremely arrogant, self-assured amateur villain like Ryder, there could be but one way out. Not for him arrest, trial, sentence, prison. Not for him disgrace, odium, humiliation.

For a moment Ryder hesitated. Then he acted without warning. He grabbed Gladys Lee by the shoulders and pushed her roughly from his path. He knocked the Major back against one of the overstuffed armchairs. And before anyone could guess his intention he ran straight across the room, and crashed through the wide window to the street eight stories below.

The silence was horrified. The receptionist screamed. Sergeant Drew reached automatically for the phone. The constable started towards the window, then the door. The two lawyers stood aghast. David Taylor wiped his palm across his forehead, his thoughts tumbling. Maybe it was for the best. No need for Gladys Lee or the Major to tell their stories in open court. No fear of publicity to harm Jean Aubyn's husband. Only he himself was unlikely to benefit, thought the Chief Inspector. He could hear Harris's comments now.

Gladys Lee had gone white, and the Major put his arm round her shoulders. It was she who asked the last questions. Through her tears she looked accusingly at David Taylor, her new spectacles slightly askew. 'You said it was a chance too good to miss,' she choked. 'Did you plan . . . ? Did you think for a moment . . . ?'

'No. No,' said Taylor. 'I didn't . . . I couldn't . . . I'm sorry, Miss Lee.'